M000190927

COUNTDOWN
TO
Christmas

USA TODAY BESTSELLING AUTHOR
BETTY SHREFFLER

COUNTDOWN TO CHRISTMAS

Copyright © 2019 by Betty Shreffler

All rights reserved. Except for use in any review, the reproduction or utilization of this work in whole or in part in any form by any electronic, mechanical, or other means, now known or hereinafter invented, including xerography, photocopying, and recording or in any information storage or retrieval system is forbidden without the written permission of the publisher. For information email: bettyshreffler@yahoo.com

This is a work of fiction. Names, characters, places, and incidents are either the product of the author's imagination or are used fictitiously, and any resemblance to actual persons, living or dead, business establishments, events, or locales is entirely coincidental.

Editor: Sandy Ebel, Personal Touch Editing

https://www.facebook.com/PersonalTouchEditing/

Proofreader: Karen Lawson

❀ Created with Vellum

CHAPTER 1

Outside my boss's office window usually is a spectacular view. In the midst of the winter weather, the snow is falling heavily from a dull gray sky, coating the ground in a fluffy white blanket. If the staff doesn't leave soon, we'll all be stuck in this office for days, sharing cooler water and this morning's dried donuts.

Mick walks back into his office, and I drag my gaze from the window, setting the file I arrived with on his desk.

"Thank you, Sophia."

"You're welcome." Dropping into the smaller chair across the desk from him, I swing one leg over the other and lean back comfortably.

Mick and I have been working together for six years. I'm the budget analyst for his personally grown business. I was one of the first staff members he brought on, so you can say I'm equally invested as he is, which has made us great friends.

"I hear Jaxson is looking for a place to live." Dropping his glasses down the bridge of his nose, he flashes his green eyes at me over the rim of them. "Aren't you in need of a roommate?"

Just hearing Jaxson's name stirs an uncontrollable tingle between my legs. The man is stunning—the tall, dark-haired, and handsome kind and the make-you-scream-multiple-O's-and-never-call-you-again kind. No matter how much my body begged to have him touching it, I've never given into the impulses. I have a heart and like to keep it well protected.

"I am, but Jaxson isn't the kind of roommate I'm looking for."

Mick stacks several documents in order and stuffs them in a manila folder. Placing them in a drawer, he returns his attention to me with a brow raised.

"Oh, what kind of roommate are you looking for?"

"Not one who will be bringing a different girl home every week to my apartment and make me have to sleep with earplugs, so I don't have to hear all the moaning."

My foot is bouncing in unison with my irritation. Mick's gaze snaps to my legs, and I frown, dropping my heel to the floor.

"Why does it bother you so much that the guy is single and enjoys it?"

Mick and I might be friends, but he is thirteen

years older and happily married with three kids. I, on the other hand, am single, no kids, no pets, and only months away from reaching the big 3-0 birthday. Truthfully, Jaxson's sex life is none of my business, but I know why his lifestyle irritates me so much. When Mick first hired him, I was smitten. I fantasized about the way it would feel to be kissed by him. I imagined him being amazing in bed and giving such incredible pleasure, I'd see stars. We flirted often, and I couldn't help wondering if he ever fisted his cock and stroked it, thinking about me. That thought alone got me through several vibrator sessions.

That all came to a screeching halt when I was leaving work late one evening and heard sounds of greedy pleasure coming from his office. With a peek inside, I discovered him banging a pretty brunette on his desk. Not one of our staff, but someone who had come to see him at work, and he'd taken the opportunity to fulfill one or both of their fantasies.

Seeing the look on his face as he came inside the woman obliterated all my hopeful fantasies. I nixed all flirting and kept my distance. It didn't take him long to notice he'd been put squarely in the friend zone, and that's where he's stayed ever since. Over the last three years, I've watched countless women come and go, none seeming to last more than a few weeks, some of them, not even a few days. Despite my distaste for his dating habits, I try not to reveal how much it actually bothers me. That doesn't stop him from giving his opinion on every guy I date though.

He's boring. He's a loud chewer. He's not good enough for you.

He always finds something wrong with every one of them. His opinion shouldn't matter to me, but it does. Every time Jaxson points out something wrong with the guy I'm dating, I obsess over it until it bothers me, then I end the relationship.

Mick's office door swings open, and Jaxson strolls in with a carefree lopsided grin beneath his striking hazel eyes. In a light gray, vertical striped, button-down shirt with the sleeves rolled up to his elbows and his blue slacks hugging his muscular thighs and ass like a soft, fitted glove, he looks delicious and so agonizingly tempting.

With a tip of his head and a smile flashed my direction, he reveals his singular dimple on the left side of his handsome face. Following the length of my legs, his hazel gold eyes develop a sparkle. Throwing one leg over the other, I roll my eyes at him, and he chuckles as he leans against the doorway. Mick glances between us, a smirk curling the corner of his mustached mouth.

"Website finished?" Mick asks Jaxson.

"Yeah. I added the new products and checked to ensure the checkout options worked. It's good to go."

"Great. Hopefully, the new sales promo you posted will entice clients for Christmas."

"It will," I assure him.

Mick gives me an appreciative nod, then stands from his desk and gathers his jacket off the back of his chair.

"I'm headed home to the wife and kids. You both should get out of here too. That storm is coming whether we like it or not." With his arms inside the jacket, he tucks it around his neck. "Jaxson, did you know Sophia is looking for a roommate?"

My gaze whips to Mick, followed by a scowl. The corner of his mouth raises a smidgen.

"I did not," Jaxson announces with surprise. "You didn't tell me?" He turns to me, his tone disappointed.

Mick walks past us, throwing his hand up in farewell.

"Lock it up when you're done."

The door closes behind him, and Jaxson walks in front of me, sits on Mick's desk, and stares me down with a questioning gaze.

"Why didn't you tell me you needed a roommate? This works out perfect for both of us."

My teeth pinch the inside of my mouth, and for a moment, I avoid his wounded expression.

"You know I'm not a fan of your dating lifestyle."

Jaxson tilts his head, his mouth quirked in disappointment.

"I wouldn't bring dates back to our place if it bothers you."

Our place. Why do those two words have to cause an emotional response?

"I don't think it's a good idea. I like our friendship the way it is. What if we ruin it by working and living together? What if we drive each other crazy?"

"We'll find ways to compromise. Come on, Soph, it'll be fun." He throws his hands out toward me. "Popcorn, movie nights, you make your delicious chocolate chip cookies, and I'll eat them."

A smile tugs the corner of my mouth, and he puts the charm on to seal the deal.

"I'll throw in a foot rub once a month and cook us dinner."

"Fine," I cave.

He's relentless. I'd have to hear his propositions and all the reasons we should live together for days until I gave in. I might as well save myself the agony.

"I'm holding you to the rule of not bringing dates back to our apartment though."

There's a smirk that plays at the corner of his mouth, then he bites his bottom lip between his teeth and my lady bits ignite at the way his eyes glisten with mischief.

"Then you can't either."

"What? It's my apartment."

"No," Jaxson shakes his head. "It'll be *our* apartment," he corrects. "And I don't want to deal with the fools you'd bring home any more than you want to deal with the women I would."

Throwing my hands in the air, I stand, heaving an

exasperated sigh. "You're already making me regret my decision."

"You know you're looking forward to having me around more often."

Rolling my eyes, I amble to the door.

"Don't flatter yourself. I tolerate you."

Jaxson steps from the desk and follows me out. Passing his office, he continues with me to mine. Inside, I shut down my computer and gather my purse and jacket while he blocks my exit.

"Don't play coy, you would miss me if I wasn't around."

With a chuckle, I shake my head at his puppy dog eyes.

"My sorrow would be short-lived."

Tucking his hands into his pockets, he laughs as he shakes his head. "You do know how to keep my ego in check, don't you?"

"Someone has to or your head would explode."

As I approach my office door, his grin is stretched across his cheeks as he turns to the side, making room for me to exit. Together, we walk to his office.

"When can I move in?"

Shutting down his computer, he gathers his favorite blue coffee mug and jacket.

"You can move in as soon as you need to. I already cleaned the spare room."

"Great, I'll start moving in tomorrow."

My eyes expand into large globes. "Are you already packed?"

As he approaches the exit, I step back for him to close the door.

"Yeah, my roommate, Clay is leaving for Colorado in three days, and once this month is up, the house is being rented to a family. I didn't want to pack or move over Christmas."

Leaving the office, I enter the code on the outside panel and wait for the light to turn red. Together, we walk through the lobby to the elevators. Down fifteen floors is the main lobby, decked out in stunning, commercially adorned Christmas trees, ornaments, and garland. It's a sight I love to see, especially after a long, tiring day. I could easily curl up on one of the lounge sofas with a cup of hot cocoa and read for hours.

That warm thought flutters away as we step out into the brisk, chilly air. A gust of wind thrusts me sideways into Jaxson's responsive arms. His coffee mug tings on the ground as he holds me steady, staring down at me, his lips inches from mine. Between us, there's a growing warmth, and it's traveling through my body, throbbing at my center as my eyes lower to his lips. Easing his grip, his hands graze my back, resting at my waist. The corner of his mouth tilts upward as he catches me staring.

"All you have to do is ask, Soph."

Pushing on his chest, I step back and gather my wits and balance.

"What are you talking about?"

Leaning over, he picks up his coffee mug and wipes the melted water off it. Looking back at me, there's a sexy, playful smirk curving his lips.

"If you're curious about what it would be like to kiss me, all you have to do is ask."

Despite the temptation teasing my body, I chuckle at his cocky smile.

"You wish, playboy. *That* will never happen."

"That's too bad," he quips.

Raising an arm, I signal an approaching taxi.

"It would never work between us." The taxi stops, and I step forward to open the door.

"Why is that?" he calls after me.

Returning my attention to him, the playfulness has left his expression, replaced by genuine curiosity.

"Because you'd break my heart."

CHAPTER 2

*W*alking into Mick's office, I stand in front of his desk, arms crossed.

"Why did you have to tell Jaxson I'm looking for a roommate? I couldn't tell him no, so now, he's moving in with me."

Taking his attention off his computer screen, he curls his index finger and thumb around his mustache as he sits back in his chair, looking humored.

"Is he really that bad? I mean, when you think of all the strange people out there, isn't Jaxson a better choice? You know him well, you're good friends, and you'll have a man you can trust living with you, which I believe is better than two young women living together alone in the city."

My arms drop to my sides, a pinch of guilt tickling my belly.

"When you say it like that, of course, it sounds like a

good idea." Turning away, I throw my hands in the air and drop into the chair. "Well, it's done. He's moving in tonight."

"That was quick."

"He's already packed. He's been looking for a place for the last couple weeks. I feel better he won't have to move over Christmas."

"That would be miserable and lonely. Now, both of you will be able to enjoy Christmas and not worry about roommates and rent."

"That's true, and it will be nice to have him around. My parents are spending Christmas in Orlando this year at their condo, so I won't be visiting them."

"Since you and Jaxson will be here for Christmas, you're welcome to come to our annual Christmas party, next Saturday at seven. There will be games, alcohol, and my wife's amazing cooking."

"Mmm, I'll be there. I'm not going to miss out on her Oreo truffles or red velvet cake. 'Tis the season for my stretchy pants."

Mick laughs as he pats his belly. "Every year, I gain five to ten pounds, eating all her amazing desserts, then spend the next eleven months working it off, only to gain it right back in December."

"You wouldn't have it any other way though, would you?"

Tilting his head back, he chuckles, and his glasses catch the light above.

"Not at all." He points my direction. "So, how is your dating life going?"

"Pitiful. The last guy I went on a date with didn't excite me at all. I'm in a dating slump."

"Why don't you give Jaxson a chance?"

"Ha! Are you kidding me? Having him as a roommate is enough. If we dated, it would be a disaster. You know he isn't one for a long-term commitment."

"He's worked here for three years. That constitutes a long-term commitment. I think he hasn't found the right woman to make him want to commit to a relationship." With a glance at his computer clock, he begins gathering items on his desk to put away for the day. "I've seen the way you two are around each other. There's chemistry."

"That's a no-go territory for me."

"Mmm-hmm." He doesn't sound convinced.

"Why are you smirking?"

"Because a single man and woman who are attracted to each other can't live together and not have sex. I give it ten days."

Coming forward in my chair, I wave my finger at him.

"No way. We can be roommates without intimacy. You watch and see. In ten days, I'll prove you wrong."

Mick places several folders into his desk drawer, then leans back in his chair, his mouth quirked.

"I bet double your Christmas bonus *you're wrong*."

He's foolish to challenge my resolve. It doesn't matter that Jaxson will be living with me. It doesn't change that I have no interest in anything more than sharing rent with him. I know not to sleep with that man. The result would be catastrophic.

"This will be an easy five hundred dollars in my pocket."

Mick chuckles as he stands and gathers his jacket.

"If you say so."

His confident sneer fuels my determination. Standing from the chair, I head toward the door.

"I'm already imagining what I can buy with that extra five hundred."

Following me out, he passes me, glancing at me sideways with that same confident smirk.

"Have a delightful Christmas vacation. Enjoy the next ten days."

CHAPTER 3

Helping Jaxson carry the last of his boxes, I set one down at the foot of his bed and blow out a breath.

"It's time for a drink. You want one?"

"Of course. What are you offering?"

"I'm starting our Christmas vacation now. I'm making Drunk Jack Frosties."

"Drunk what?" One brow rises as he stares at me in confusion.

"Come on." I wave my hand for him to follow me to the kitchen. "I'll show you how it's done."

Pulling out the blender and two stemless wine glasses, I set them aside and gather the rest of the ingredients. Pouring the vodka, champagne, blue curacao, lemonade, and ice into the blender, I press the button and wait while it turns the ingredients into an icy cocktail. While that sits, I run a lemon wedge around the rim of each glass then dip them in sanding sugar. Jaxson watches in fascination as I pour the icy mixture into the rimmed glasses. Sliding one glass toward him, I lift the other. Jaxson brings his glass toward mine.

"Thanks for giving me a place to live and for being such a good friend all these years."

Warm hazel eyes hold my gaze, the affection I see in them surprising. He's usually playful and cocky at work.

"You're welcome."

Over the rim of his glass, he watches me drink as he swallows his. Those warm hazel eyes widen, glance down at his glass, then return to me with a smile beneath them.

"This is good. Really good."

"It's an easy one too. My old roomie and I had a hobby of discovering mixed drink recipes for our movie night."

Taking another long drink, he lowers it and tips the glass toward me.

"I think we need to carry on that tradition."

"I'd like that. How about you pick out the next mixed drink, and I'll pick out the movie? She and I did cocktail movie nights on Friday if that works for you."

"It does, and I will."

"Good." Taking another drink, I nod toward his room. "Would you like help unpacking?"

"As long as you avoid the small blue box."

Setting my glass down, an impish grin curls my lips as I dash for his room, hearing his glass clink the counter as he bolts after me. Going around the island counter, he chases me down the hall and into his room. Leaning down and giggling as I reach for the box, strong arms wrap around me and scoop me up. Twirling me through the air, he lands on his back on the bed, still holding me in his arms. Laughter spills out of me as we roll around, my efforts to escape futile.

"What's in there?"

Sitting us up, he keeps hold of me. I'm still on his lap and aware of how comfortable it feels. He doesn't scoot me off or release me.

"My private things."

"Like sexual things?"

My hand is on his jean-covered thigh as his laugh rumbles his chest behind me.

"Is that what you thought was in there?"

"Yes."

Looking over my shoulder, there's a flush in his cheeks, and he's staring at my lips.

"It's not sex toys, even though I'm amused that was your first thought, you naughty girl."

"Well, I know how you are with the ladies."

I go to stand, but he pulls me back down onto his lap, and through my shirt, he caresses my stomach. Pleasured goosebumps pebble across my shoulders and arms.

"How am I with the ladies?"

"Skilled," I chuckle.

"That's true, but I don't think that's what you meant."

The liquor is warming my body, and with the added touch of his caress, I'm craving more of his touch. Before things get carried away, I peel his arms from around my waist and approach one of the boxes.

"You date more than I do, that's all."

"Mmm-hmm." His eyes narrow questioningly as his mouth twists up. "Soph, I don't sleep with every woman I go on a date with. You know that, right?"

Opening the box, I take out a stack of T-shirts and carry them to the tall dresser along the wall.

"What you do or don't do on your dates is none of my business. Which drawer?" I ask, pointing to the dresser.

"Third one down." Standing, he moves over to another box and opens it. Taking out boxers and briefs, he comes over to the dresser and puts them in the top drawer.

"I think you believe I sleep with women far more than I do."

Going back to the same box, I gather a stack of shorts, sweatpants, and flannel pajama pants, and he points to the bottom drawer.

"I don't want to know about the women you've slept with." The truth is, I don't like thinking about him sleeping with *any* woman.

"I'm not seeing anyone now, so you don't have to worry about me breaking the no-dates-over rule."

There's an excited flutter in my stomach. I shouldn't like hearing he's single that much.

"How about you? Are you dating anyone?"

He empties his box, flattens it, and sets it to the side. I hand him the empty one I have, and he starts breaking it down. Sitting on the floor, I reach for another box.

"No, my dating life has sucked lately. None of the guys I've gone out with have interested me beyond the one date."

"Why haven't we ever gone on a date?"

The shock of his question freezes my movement; my hands hold the box flaps open as I look up at him, speechless.

"When I started working for Mick three years ago, I thought there was something between us."

"I..." The memory of him thrusting into that pretty brunette flashes through my mind like it was yesterday, creating a knot in my stomach. "I thought there was too, then I happened to come to your office when you were having an office rendezvous with some chick." I finish opening the box, avoiding his expression. "After that, my interest ended."

Glancing up, I catch the shock on his face. With red cheeks, he rubs a hand over the back of his neck.

"Yeah, I can see how that would make you feel that way. I didn't know you saw me." Jaxson turns away from me, his eyes pinching closed before he reaches down and grabs another box.

"If I hadn't seen you, what would that have changed?"

"Probably nothing," he admits. "Not then, anyway. It's different now."

"How so?" Rising to my feet, I take his stack of button-down shirts on hangers over to his closet.

"Because now, I care for you."

My hand stops hanging the shirt currently in my hand. My head lowers and angles toward him as my heartbeat quickens.

"I care for you too. You're one of my best friends."

Jaxson steps into the closet doorway, blocking my exit.

"You're mine too."

Grazing his fingers over mine, he takes the hangers from my hand and hooks them on the bar. With him standing this close, his eyes centered on me, the warmth of his body and scent of his irresistible cologne assaulting my senses, the urge to feel his kiss is too much, too tempting. Putting a hand on his soft cotton shirt and firm chest, I create space and squeeze out of the closet.

"I'm going to clean up the kitchen then take a shower. You good to handle the rest?"

Jaxson's head drops, and he sucks part of his lip between his teeth. "Yeah, I'm good. Thanks for helping me move in."

"Of course. If you need anything, let me know."

The moment I leave his room, I release the breath stuck in my lungs. Body still tingling, I keep thinking about his arms around me, him standing within kissable reach. I need to be more careful. Jaxson is a slippery slope I don't want to fall down.

CHAPTER 4

*H*aving finished making eggs, wheat toast, and a morning smoothie, I tap on Jaxson's door to offer him breakfast.

"Come in."

On the other side of the door, Jaxson is on the bare hardwood floor, doing pushups in workout shorts to music pumping out of his cell phone, sweat beading across his arms and back. It looks like he's been in here doing cardio activities for a while this morning. With each up and down, his arms flex, showing off the contours of his tight, toned muscles in his arms, back, and chest. Leaning against the doorway, I suck my lip between my teeth as arousal stirs between my legs.

"What's up?"

His voice snaps me out of my daze, and I shift my feet.

"I made a high protein breakfast, and from the

looks of your workout routine, that's probably what you want."

"That's perfect."

Using his fists as leverage, he brings his legs toward his knees and stands. Grabbing a towel that's draped over the wooden footboard of his bed, he uses it to wipe the sweat off his face and the back of his neck. When he catches me staring, his mouth tilts sideways.

"I'll take a shower, then be out."

"Sounds good."

Sitting with my leg propped up on my white-washed dining chair, I watch the strangers pass by on the sidewalk below, my smoothie in hand, and half empty. Jaxson enters the dining room in a pair of worn, comfortable-looking jeans and a graphic T-shirt that says:

Bucket List

1. Beer

2. Ice

Humored, my mouth curls, and I lower my leg to face him as he sits down in the chair opposite me. My table is a small, two-seat table next to the largest window in the apartment with a view of other buildings, and in the far-right corner, a glimpse of the city park. Around the window, I've hung flowerpots with dangling plants that give the apartment a lively, whimsical look and lift my mood.

"Breakfast might be a little cold."

Jaxson gathers the fork and digs in, shrugging a shoulder.

"I don't mind."

After a forkful of eggs, he lifts the smoothie cup.

"What's in it?"

"My own concoction. Spinach, kale, ginger root. Things like that. It'll give you energy that'll last all day."

Jaxson tips the cup and takes several swallows, finishing half the drink.

"Not bad. If you show me what to put in it, I'll take turns making it in the morning."

"I think having you as a roommate is going to work out."

"Good." Jaxson leans back in his chair, stretching out his legs as he smiles. "I want it to work out."

His half-cocked grin creates a tingle in my belly. I feel warmth flooding my cheeks and look away. Lifting my drink, I empty the glass.

"Do you have any plans today?"

"I don't. I'm unpacked, so I'm free. Do you have something in mind?"

"I'd like to put up my Christmas tree and decorate it. You want to help?"

Leaning forward, he rests his arms on the table. Below his T-shirt sleeve, his biceps flex, and I notice— too well.

"I can't promise I'll do a good job, but yeah, I'd like to help."

After a quick clean up, he follows me to the storage

closet between our rooms, and I drag out my Christmas tree box and two more boxes of ornaments and garland. Jaxson goes into the kitchen, retrieves a knife, and cuts the tape I have over the box. When it pops open, he chuckles at the white fluff that flies out, landing on his shirt and pants, remaining there like tiny, puffy ornaments.

"I think we're done here. The tree is decorated."

Giggling, I join him and start picking off the fluff balls. He watches me with fascination as I laugh and dust off his shirt.

"I love your laugh."

My hand stops, and I glance up at him, seeing the affection in his eyes.

"Every time I hear you laugh in your office it makes me smile."

I don't know what to say. I'm imagining his handsome face smiling in his office when he hears me and the vision creates a flutter in my stomach.

"I do the same thing when I hear yours. You and Mick must talk about some interesting things. I hear you two laugh a lot when you're in his office."

"We do. He tells me things he probably doesn't tell you."

"Like what?"

Returning to the box on the floor, I sit down with my legs crossed while Jaxson finishes opening the tree box and pulls out the bottom of the tree. More white fluff scatters on the floor and sticks to his clothing, but he doesn't care. He continues taking everything out and lays it in order of how he's going to stack it.

"Funny things his kids do and…"

"And?" I press.

"Some stuff about his married sex life. You can't tell him I told you this." He gives me a pointed look, and it sucks me in even more.

"What?"

"He and his wife are into some interesting role-playing."

"No way!" Chuckling, my mouth tilts. "Like what?"

Jaxson puts the tree frame and bottom layer together as he laughs.

"Like costumes and toys. Nurse and doctor. Firefighter and damsel in distress. Veterinarian and dog."

My eyes widen as my stomach rolls with laughter. "Veterinarian and dog? Who was the dog?"

Jaxson looks at me sideways, his own smile widening as he watches me in a fit of laughter.

"His wife wore the collar."

"Oh!"

Jaxson reaches for the middle tree section. "Crazy, right? But they have a good time, and it spices things up for them."

"I won't be able to look at him the same!"

"You'll have to. We did *not* have this conversation." With a raised brow, he shoots me a stern look.

"I won't say a word. I'll just be giggling every time I look at him for a week or so."

Jaxson sets the final section of the tree on the top as I open the first ornament box.

"Where do you want it?"

"In the corner there." I point past the couch, between the electric fireplace on the wall and the large window on the right.

Leaning down, he reaches into the branches, gathers the plastic trunk near the bottom and top, then carries the six-foot tree the few feet over. Picking up the box, I join him.

"Have you ever done anything like that?"

"Role-playing?" he laughs. "Not like that. I've enjoyed some toys and accessories, but not any costumes or character play."

Pulling out the garland, I hand him the bundle as I search for the end.

"What kind of toys and accessories?"

His brow lifts.

"You really want to know?"

Curiosity might get me into trouble, but I'm too invested to turn back now.

"Yes."

"Scarves, ties, cuffs, and a few other things."

"What are some of those other things?"

Jaxson watches me, studying my features. Whatever he's thinking makes him grin.

"Vibrators, other sex toys, lotions, whipped cream, chocolate syrup."

I bite my lip, and his gaze goes straight to my mouth.

"Have you ever used any of those?" The color in his eyes seems a shade darker, glossier, and I'm almost certain this is what he looks like when he's aroused—carnal, sexy, and damn near irresistible.

"Yes."

"What things have you used?"

"Just about all of those."

He rakes a hand down his face, his eyes widening.

"You know that's hot, right? Not all women are adventurous in the bedroom."

Finding the end of the garland, I tuck it into the lower branches and begin winding it around the tree.

"Sounds like you like sexually adventurous women."

"I do. Anything wrong with that?"

"Not at all. There are women who enjoy being with a sexually adventurous man."

Jaxson follows me around the tree, feeding me garland as we circle around it.

"Do you?"

Moving back a step, I catch his lascivious stare.

"Yes."

There's a pause before he stuffs the bundle of garland from his hands into the tree.

"I can't do this anymore."

My brows pinch inward. "Can't do what?"

"Pretend we don't want each other."

A solid hand wraps around my waist, pulling me to him as his lips crash into mine. Any thoughts are obliterated the moment my body ignites, his dominant masculinity and need drawing out my desire. Lifting my legs, he turns us, putting me against the wall. Arousal throbs at my center, my body betraying me with its aching need for him. Pressing his erection against me, I moan into his mouth, and he pushes harder, giving my body more of what it wants. Clasping my hands in his, he pins them to the wall as his thrusts continue, tipping my need for him from pleasure to sweet agony.

"Your room or mine?"

Those words drag me down from my clouded bliss.

"We can't."

Pushing at his chest, he allows my legs to drop and keeps an arm around me as his brows dip, and the lines around his mouth tighten.

"What's wrong?"

"I don't want to ruin our friendship. All it takes is one night, then it'll get awkward between us."

The caress of his hand along my cheek kindles the arousal between my legs. My body is too needy for his touch, too quick to surrender.

"It doesn't have to be like that."

"I don't want a friend with benefits arrangement. I'm sorry."

Stepping away from him, I hear him release a

weighted sigh behind me. Going into my room, I close the door and lean against it. Sliding down the frame, I curl my knees to my chest. For years, I've wanted him, but all I ever wanted was to be the only woman he was interested in. After watching the women come and go, I knew I would never be more than an office fling, and my heart would never heal from that.

Tears fill my eyes, wishing I hadn't let him room with me or let the kiss go as far as it did. Now he knows how much my body wants him, and now, I'll have to be more careful.

CHAPTER 5

*A*fter a couple hours reading an eBook in bed, I leave my bedroom to pee and find Jaxson sprawled out on the couch with a paperback book in his hand. Lowering the book, he watches me go into the kitchen and put water in the tea kettle.

"Are you still mad at me?"

After turning the stove on, I pass the Christmas boxes and sit in the armchair next to the couch. He's giving me those puppy dog eyes that always win my forgiveness.

"I'm not mad at you. You mean a lot to me. I don't want to lose my best friend, awesome new roommate, and favorite co-worker over meaningless sex."

A frown pulls at his lips below the hurt in his eyes.

"Is that what you think? That you don't mean anything to me?"

"I know you care about me as a friend, but it's

30

different for women. We get emotionally invested when we have sex. It's easier for men to have sex with no strings."

Swinging his legs over the edge of the couch, he sets the book next to him.

"Come here." Taking hold of my wrist, he tugs me out of the chair, and with a hand on my hip, he lowers me onto the couch with my legs dangling over his.

"I don't want to do anything that upsets you or ruins our friendship either. You mean more to me than you realize. I get that you don't want to have sex, and I respect that, but I still want us to be comfortable around each other... and maybe kiss every once in a while." A wolfish grin curls the corner of his mouth.

"You're incorrigible." Laughing, I tap his chest.

Leaning his head back on the cushion, he caresses my cheek and slides a strand of my hair behind my ear.

"That was one of the hottest kisses I've ever had. I can't help wanting to feel that way again." Grazing his thumb over my lips, my mouth parts as arousal surges between my legs. "How did it make you feel?"

The memory of his kiss has left its mark on my body, and right now, it's remembering how it felt... vividly. My words stick in my throat as intense need courses through me. As I look back at him, my gaze passes between his stunning hazel eyes and the mouth that gave me overwhelming pleasure.

"It was better than I imagined."

The side of his mouth rises.

"You've imagined us kissing?"

With each of his caresses through my hair, my body melts farther into his arms.

"Yes."

"Is that all you imagined?"

"No."

Caressing his other hand along the outside of my thigh, he grips my leg and brings me closer to his chest.

"Tell me what else you imagined about us."

His lips are agonizingly close, so close, my lips burn with a desire desperate to be satisfied.

"I don't think that is something I should tell you."

As his palm kneads my outer thigh, I close my eyes, indulging in the pleasure of his caress.

"I'll tell you what I imagined if you tell me first."

Moving his hand to my inner thigh, his thumb applies pressure as he massages my leg.

"I've imagined—"

The tea kettle whistles, and my gaze flicks to it. Putting my hand on his chest, I step off the couch. With colored cheeks and a tense jaw, he puts an arm behind the back of his head and drops it on the couch cushion as he closes his eyes.

Our conversation was affecting him as much as it was me, and clearly, he didn't want it to end. Putting a tea bag in a mug, I add water and a spoonful of honey. Jaxson comes into the kitchen and gets a mug for himself. Dipping a spoon into the jar of honey, he eyes me sideways.

"Our conversation isn't over."

"We still have a tree to finish."

"All right. I'll help you finish decorating the tree." Scooping a dollop of honey on his finger, he brings it to my mouth. When I lick the honey off, his lips curve. "Then, you finish telling me what you imagined about us."

"I'm not making any promises." With a wink, I gather my mug and head into the living room. He follows me in and sets his mug on the coffee table.

"I guess I need to do a hell of a job decorating this tree. Maybe then, you'll reward me."

"Let's see how well you do, stud."

Setting my mug next to his, I sit down in front of the ornament box and take them out while he finishes putting the gold garland on the tree. Every so often, I catch him watching me. When he finishes, he sits next to me, putting a hand on my leg.

"Are any of the ornaments special to you?"

"These are." Picking up a set of four shiny green and gold, glittery bulbs, I hand them to him. "I've had these since I was a kid. They were the first ones I picked out when my parents said I could choose my first fancy bulbs."

"Then, these are the ones we'll put on first."

Taking my hand in his, he pulls me up. Holding the bulbs, he hands me one at a time to hang on the tree. With the next box, I hand them to him, one by one. With my favorite bulbs now glistening as they dangle from the tree branches, we gather the remaining bulbs and try to place them evenly. As I place the last bulb, I stretch on my tippy toes to put it higher on the tree. His fingers graze over my hand, taking the bulb and placing it for me. As I lower on my toes, he kisses my cheek, sending a sensation of pleasure across my arms.

"I enjoyed this. I think the tree looks nice."

"I do too."

Jaxson goes to the back of the tree and plugs it in. I step back and admire all the pretty lights and sparkling ornaments, my smile stretching across my face.

"You look really happy."

"I am. It's so pretty. Thank you for helping me."

"Thanks for asking me."

Sitting on the couch, he lifts his mug of tea and relaxes. Gathering mine, I sit next to him and stare at the tree. Putting an arm around my shoulders, he plays with my hair, and I lean into him.

"It's nice seeing you this happy."

"The Christmas tree is one of my favorite things about Christmas. It gets me in the spirit. Speaking of, what would you like for Christmas?"

"You don't have to get me anything. You gave me a place to live."

"That doesn't count. So, tell me what you'd like."

"I have a wish list on Amazon. Does that help?"

"It does. I can shop for you without you knowing exactly what I'm getting you."

Taking a sip of my tea, I look back at the tree.

Caressing my cheek, he draws my attention back to him, his mouth curving when my eyes meet his.

"What do you want for Christmas?"

I snigger, and his brows pinch inward. "What?"

"A real relationship." I frown. "I'm tired of being alone."

"I don't understand how you're single."

"What do you mean?"

"You're funny, fun to be around, smart, and beautiful."

Heat warms my cheeks as his eyes roam my face.

"Thank you. That means a lot coming from you."

Taking mine, he sets both mugs on the coffee table. With his arm back around my shoulder, he runs his fingers through my hair, and gathers my hand in his free hand. Sitting like this, him giving me affection, creates the kind of feelings I'm afraid of—feelings I know will lead to heartache.

"I should make dinner."

"It's still early."

"We skipped lunch."

"You're avoiding telling me."

Biting my lip, I chuckle. "That's true."

"I want to know."

"It's better if we don't go there."

"Soph."

I blow out a breath.

"I imagined being the one you fucked on your desk.

35

Then that fantasy became a reality, except it wasn't me."

Withdrawing my hand from his, I go into the kitchen. Distracting myself, I ignore the knot in my stomach and focus on gathering ingredients for dinner. Jaxson comes into the kitchen and leans on the island counter with his chin against his closed hands.

"You liked me a lot back then, didn't you?"

"Yep."

Avoiding looking at him, I start chopping vegetables.

"I ruined it, didn't I?"

"Yep."

"You stopped flirting and talking to me. I thought you weren't interested, so I moved on."

With tense shoulders, I keep chopping the carrots.

"Nope. I was interested, but after seeing you with someone else, I realized we didn't feel the same way."

Glancing over my shoulder, I see him drop his head into his hands and exhale.

"I'm sorry, Soph. I didn't mean to hurt you."

"I don't think you did, but you also didn't intend for me to see you fucking that chick. If I hadn't, I would've been just another notch on the figurative belt." I stop chopping and look at him. "So really, you saved me from an unwanted heartache."

Jaxson shrugs his shoulders. "So, it doesn't matter what I would've done. I was an asshole for not having sex with you, and I would've been an asshole if I had sex with you."

Turning to face him, frustration builds in my chest, tightening it.

"It wasn't about sex. I liked you a lot and thought something was growing between us. Yeah, seeing you with her made me jealous, but it also made me realize I didn't want to be her because a week later, she came back by, and you blew her off. Commitment isn't your thing. I'm glad I learned that early on."

Jaxson's jaw ticks, and he pushes off the counter to walk away.

"I blew her off because I noticed a change in you, and it bothered me. When I realized it was because I had feelings for you, I ended it with her to pursue you. But you put me in the friend zone and made it clear I wasn't good enough for you."

"So it's my fault I saw you banging that chick and lost interest?"

"There's no point in continuing this discussion. I know where I stand." Jaxson gathers his jacket and shoes by the door. "I'm going out for dinner."

The door closes behind him, and it takes all of my focus to keep my hands steady. Chopping slower, I fight back tears.

Moving the chicken, rice, and vegetables around on my plate, I give up trying to eat. My stomach is in knots, and I'm worried about Jaxson going out late with the bad weather. When he does come back, I'm worried about how awkward it will be between us. Maybe sex would've been easier than the argument we just had. Going into the kitchen, I put the leftovers in a container, then return the Christmas boxes to storage. After a shower, I lie in bed, reading, but I don't make it through many pages. My mind keeps going back to our argument and the knowledge he shared about wanting to pursue me. I guess it wasn't meant to be, and that's probably for the best. I know it wouldn't have worked out. Eventually, he would've lost interest in me.

The front door opens, and I set my book aside to listen. Boots thud on the floor, then his footsteps traipse through the apartment and stop outside my door. They start to walk away, and my heart sinks. A moment later, they return, and my door opens. Jaxson walks in quietly and lies on the opposite side of the bed. I turn the nightstand lamp on as he gathers the pillow next to mine, tucks it in his arms, facing me.

"I don't want us to be upset with each other."

I tuck my pillow in my arms and face him. The sorrow in his eyes tightens the knots in my belly.

"I don't either."

"The thought of losing you bothered me a lot. I ended up in a bar and had a few drinks to take the edge off."

"I couldn't eat dinner. I was miserable the whole time you were gone."

"I'm sorry I fucked up back then."

"I shouldn't have been so jealous. We were just friends who hadn't done anything more than flirt."

"Will you forgive me?"

With hope and sorrow visible in his sleepy eyes, it pulls at my heart.

"Yes."

Reaching out, he takes my hand in his warm, strong one.

"Soph," he whispers, his eyelids drooping.

"Yeah?"

"I love you."

With closed eyes, he drifts off to sleep, and I lie there, struggling through a multitude of emotions. What does *I love you* mean to him? Will he remember he said it tomorrow? Will he remember this conversation? Have I kept him at arm's length for the wrong reasons? Did I make a mistake shutting him out?

CHAPTER 6

*W*aking up to an empty bed creates a hollow pit in my stomach. Part of me wishes he was still lying next to me, part wonders if it was a wishful dream, and the last part is dreading leaving my bedroom. But I do anyway, and after brushing my teeth and putting my hair in a messy bun, I traipse into the kitchen. Jaxson is there with a spread of healthy foods on the counter and the blender sitting out. My mouth curves as I watch him read my recipe card. When he sees me enter the kitchen, he sets the card down and hugs me.

"I don't like fighting with you. Let's not do that again."

Being held against his warm, firm chest is comforting and soothes away the nerves I had knotting in my stomach. Putting my arms around him, I rub his back, and he squeezes me a little tighter. Kissing my head, he releases me and immediately, I want his arms back.

"I didn't like it either. It made me feel awful."

"Me too. Our friendship is important to me. I hope we can let go of what happened in the past." Taking my hand in his, he caresses his thumb over the top of mine. "Can we do that?"

The answer was yes, the moment he asked. With hope filling his eyes, it cements what I already felt.

"Of course."

Leaning down, he kisses my cheek, and my body leans toward him as warmth spreads through it.

"Do I have everything we need for the smoothie?"

Looking at the counter, I take inventory. "Yeah, you do."

Standing next to him, I help him chop and load the blender. Bumping my hip, he gets my attention and smiles at me.

"What do you think about making cookies tonight?"

Chuckling, the corner of my mouth lifts. "I bake, you eat?"

"I don't know what I'm doing, but I can try to help."

"I'll show you how it's done."

"Sounds good."

He presses the blender, and it buzzes and spins. Taking two cups out of the cupboard, I hold them while he pours.

"I'm going out for a while. I got an idea of something I want to get you."

Hazel eyes look into mine, awaiting my reaction.

"What is it?"

Grazing his finger under my chin, he raises it.

"I can't tell you. It's a good surprise."

Anxious energy bundles in my belly. He's come up with something good, I can tell. I want my present for him to be just as good.

"I'm dying to know what it is."

Raising the cup, he winks behind the rim of the glass.

"You'll love it. I promise."

"I'm going shopping for you too."

"Where?" Leaning against the counter, he finishes the smoothie.

"The mall. I have some ideas and want to check them out."

"All right. Good. I'll see you tonight."

Setting the cup in the dishwasher, he closes it, kisses me on the cheek, and heads to his room. Touching my cheek, I linger in the kitchen, biting my lip as my body still tingles from his affection.

The mall is packed, but the decorations are beautiful. I sit by the massive woodland Christmas tree in the center, drink a chai tea, and make a list of everyone I need to shop for. Jaxson isn't the only one. My work ethic might be on point, but I'm a terrible procrastinator when it comes to Christmas shopping. It's always a struggle for me because I want every gift to be perfect.

It takes several stores and three different purchases until I'm happy with my gifts for Jaxson. They're still not as heartfelt as I would've liked, but I think I chose the right kind of gifts for him. It's almost time for dinner when I return to my apartment with both hands full of bags. Pushing through the door, I hear Jaxson in the hall. The conversation he's having slows my steps. Standing still, I listen.

"I just moved in a couple of days go. She is," he laughs. "She's beautiful… No, I haven't told her. It's not the right time." His voice trails off as he goes farther down the hall and into his room, closing the door behind him.

Several questions filter through my mind, leaving me confused and anxious, wanting to know what he hasn't told me. Setting the bags down, I remove my jacket and shoes, then quietly gathering my bags, I head toward my room. He walks out of his door and stops abruptly before smacking into me. Putting his hands on my shoulders, he keeps me from toppling over.

"Let me help you."

"Thank you."

Gathering bags from one hand, he follows me into my room. As soon as we step inside, I stop, eyes wide, gazing around my room. While I was gone, he decorated it—gold and white stars dangle from the ceiling, white lights arch around the window, and there're twinkling candles on each nightstand.

My heartbeat quickens as I stand there, breathless. It's beautiful, creative, and incredibly sweet. Setting the bags down, I hug him, and he holds me in his arms, caressing my back, strengthening the affection that's growing for him.

"I love it."

Happy tears brim my eyes, and he cups my face in his hands. Between us is heat I can't deny. He lowers his mouth to mine, and I accept him, wanting the rush his kiss gives my body. With one hand around my back, his other curls in my hair as he brings us close together, his sensual kiss tingling my nerve endings.

For several minutes, we kiss, tasting and teasing, tangled in each other's arms, and I don't want it to end. As the heat builds at my center, I push into him, craving more. His hand lowers to my ass, squeezes and tugs me to him as he moans into my mouth. When his erection presses into me, he withdraws, leaving me breathless, my lips prickling with want.

"I'm sorry. You cripple my self-control."

Hearing how I affect him gives me a sense of satisfaction. I shouldn't like having that control over him, but I do.

Placing his thumb on my bottom lip, he presses and slides it down, watching my eyes as he does it.

"I don't want to stop kissing you, but I will if you tell me to."

My body grows warmer, my desire to feel his lips stronger.

"I don't want you to."

Taking my hand, he leads me to my bed. Sitting on the edge, he places me between his legs, puts his hands on my hips, massages them, then lower, cupping my ass. With the pressure of his hands, I come forward, straddling his lap.

"No sex."

"No sex," he agrees.

Lying back, he takes me with him, his arms wrapped around my back as he brings his lips back to mine. The way his hands move in unison with the sensual caress of his lips blurs my surroundings and ignites a fiery need I can't control. My desire yearns to be sated, and with every stroke of his hands, it's a battle I'm losing. Between my lips, his skilled tongue dances with mine, a tango of torment and lust I'm lost to.

Wrapping a palm around my ass, he flips us, pushing his erection against me, eliciting a breathy, pleasured moan. Watching me with his erotic gaze, he unbuttons my jeans and trails a finger down my underwear. Kissing below my belly button, he tucks his fingers into my jeans, removing them from my hips and legs. A warm breath blows over the thin piece of fabric covering me, and I tilt my head back as pleasure drives me over the edge. My need for more is dangerous, my will shattering.

Rubbing his hand over my underwear, he teases my

clit, applying pressure and circling it. My body trembles with desire so strong, I'm afraid I'll come soon. As if he senses it, he slides my underwear off, spreads my legs, and lowers his mouth to my clit. Working the sensitive bundle of nerves, he licks slow and soft, a sensual torture before his pressure increases, and his tongue lowers, invading my opening. He tongue fucks me into ecstasy, my body shaking, my desire reaching its peak, plunging me over the other side.

I lie there, pleasure rippling throughout my body, expecting we're finished. That thought is obliterated as his fingers slide into me, stroking in and out, finding his way to my G-spot. My hips rock toward him as I moan with renewed desire. Finding the spot, he holds my hip steady, working me into a frenzy as I chase another orgasm. Gripping my hand over his, I keep his pace and position, my head falling back as I come on his hand.

"Damn, you're beautiful."

Unfastening his jeans, he drops down on the bed, holding himself above me. Taking my hand, he slides it into his open jeans, putting it on his rock-hard erection. Taking control, I fist his length, the feel of his thick cock reigniting my arousal. Pushing on his chest, I flip him over and lower to his waist. My movement surprises him, and he stares down at me with an erotic gaze that longs for more.

Putting my mouth around his cock, I hold the base

and stroke up and down and put as much of him in my mouth as I can. A groan of relief leaves his mouth as he puts an arm behind his head and the other hand in my hair.

"Yes, like that," he encourages. "Fuck, that feels good."

My head bobs up and down as I suck hard, wanting to give the same pleasure he gave me. As his fist grips my hair and he moans, I know he likes what I'm doing. Pushing him farther back in my throat, I take him deeper, and his moans grow louder.

"I'm gonna come."

He's giving me the chance to pull away and not swallow, but I remain there, and he fists my hair tightly as he releases into my mouth.

Dropping his head back, he lays an arm over his eyes and exhales. Bringing it back down, he lifts his head to look at me. Wrapping his hand around my arm, he lays me above his chest.

"That was better than I imagined. You make me feel good." Gathering a fallen strand of hair, he puts it behind my ear. "Really good."

"You make me feel the same way. I've never had an orgasm that fast."

Lowering me down to his lips, he kisses me.

"I'm glad you told me. I like knowing I can pleasure you like that."

With his hand caressing my face and hair, he holds my gaze to his, the affection I see in his eyes confusing my heart and mind. One wants to be reasonable and protective while the other wants to keep falling.

"Do you still want to make cookies?"

With a chuckle, I splay my fingers over his chest and lift myself off him.

"Yes, I do."

"I want to help."

When I stand, he comes up behind me, moves my hair off one shoulder to the other one. Goosebumps pebble along my arms as he places a tender kiss in the nook of my neck and shoulder. Leaning down, he gathers my underwear and jeans. Pulling my nude, seamless underwear out of my jeans, his mouth cocks sideways as he twirls them on his finger.

"You should make cookies in just that sweater."

Laughing, I reach for the underwear, and he pulls them back.

"I'll get cold."

"Wear those knee-high stockings you wore the other day. I couldn't stop thinking about you with nothing but them on."

A gasp of shock parts my open mouth, and he laughs. Tossing my underwear and jeans on the bed, he moves toward my closet.

"Where are they?"

Zipping his jeans, he walks into my closet and turns the light on. Following him in, I stand in the doorway watching him open drawers, searching.

"They're in that drawer." I point, and he opens it, then pulls out a gray pair with black lace at the top.

"Wear these."

Snatching them from his hand, I blow out a puff of air, hiding my smile.

"You're not going to let me wear underwear, are you?"

"Nope." He winks. "You can try, and I'll enjoy stripping you out of them. Either way, it's a win-win for me."

I bite my lip to keep from smiling. "Fine."

Going to the bed, I scrunch one knee-high stocking down and slip my leg into it. Jaxson leans against the wall, watching me as I slide it up my leg. When I do the second, he exhales, his cheeks gaining color. Standing from the bed, I leave my bedroom and he follows. As we walk out of my bedroom, his hand slips below my long sweater and squeezes a bare ass cheek. I squeal and turn toward him. Putting a hand around the back of my neck, he smothers my squeal with his lips.

"I like you like this." Those sensuous hazel eyes stare into mine. Biting my bottom lip, he slips a hand between my legs, arousing me with the stroke of his fingers. "I like having access."

Tugging at the button of his jeans, I pluck it free, rubbing at the growing swell of his cock.

"It's not fair. I don't have easy access."

Jaxson closes his eyes, his jaw tightening as I stroke

him. When he opens his eyes, there's a spark of mischief.

"I'll remedy that."

Lifting his shirt off, he tosses it through the open door of his room. Stripping out of his jeans, he throws them after his shirt. He's standing in front of me with tight muscles and broad shoulders, gray briefs fitted to his narrow waist. Taking my hand, he slips it into the opening, filling it with his stretched cock.

"It's just a pocket away."

As I stroke his erection, he moves closer, and my back hits the wall. Eliminating the space between us, he covers my body with his. Raising my sweater to my hips, he kisses along my neck, and my traitorous body begs for more.

"We have to slow down." Just saying the words tightens my chest and dries my mouth. I stop stroking him, and he groans next to my ear.

"Are you sure you want to? Your hand is still wrapped around my cock."

Reluctantly, I open my palm. Looking down at his freed erection, I bite my lip at the rush of arousal. With how thick and long he is, I know he'd feel amazing.

"What are you thinking?"

"That I want you, but I don't know what this is between us."

With his hand cupping my jaw, he grazes his thumb along my lips and cheek.

"I think this is what we've both wanted and have never given it a chance."

Tears moisten my eyes as my stomach knots.

"I don't want to fall for you and end up heartbroken."

Placing his head against mine, his hand caresses up and down my arm.

"I'm not going to hurt you."

"You don't know that."

"I need you to trust me."

"I'm willing to, but I want to take things slow."

Tucking his fading erection back into his briefs, he kisses my cheek.

"Then we'll go slow."

Putting his fingers through mine, he leads me into the kitchen. Bringing me in front of him, he swings his arms around me, hugging my back to his chest as he kisses my shoulder.

"What do we need to make your delicious chocolate chip cookies?"

Telling him the ingredients, I point to the cabinet where he can find most of them. He sets them on the counter as I gather the mixing bowls. Reaching for my recipe card box against the wall, I bring it forward and sort to the spot where I keep my grandmother's recipe card. Pulling it out, I set it to the side where he can read it. While he measures out the first ingredient, I turn on the stove.

Stepping back, I watch him in his boxer briefs

mixing baking ingredients. As he moves, his muscles flex, and I squeeze my legs at the arousal that's awakening. With his side profile, I admire his angled jaw and sinful lips. He's strikingly attractive, something I've always felt, but in these last two days, I'm seeing more than the good-looking, cocky playboy I've labeled him to be. He's shown patience, how caring he is, and an interest in doing things I like. He's asked me to trust him and I truly want to give him that chance. The only problem with asking to go slow is every time we're intimate, I crave more. How long can I keep things going slow when my body reacts to him the way it does?

Jaxson eyes me sideways and grins.

"Like what you see?"

"Yes."

Joining him, I put my arm through his and raise my chin to accept his kiss.

"How am I doing?"

"The mixture has the right color and texture. Now it's time to add the flour and chocolate chips."

"All right. I'm not screwing up so far."

"No, you're doing great."

I rub his arm, and he looks down at me with adoration that curls my lips.

"What?"

"You're stunning."

"You're making me blush."

"I know. I like it."

My smile grows as I dump the flour and chocolate chips into the bowl, then he gathers the bowl and stirs. Once it's the right consistency, I hand him a spoon, and we scoop out large spoonfuls to put on the cookie sheet. Placing the cookie sheet in the oven, I set the timer for ten minutes.

Jaxson comes into my space, putting his arms around my waist. Lifting me, I giggle as he props me up on the island counter. With his finger and thumb on my jaw, he brings me forward for a kiss. My legs spread with him between them and he eyes me with a devilish grin as he slides my sweater up my thighs.

"I have ten minutes."

"Ten minutes for what?" I play coy.

"To give you another orgasm."

Spreading his fingers between my breasts, he applies pressure and lays me on my back. Throwing my left leg over his shoulder, he spreads the other wider. Cool air meets my opening before the warmth of his tongue fills it.

Reaching down, I curl my fingers into his hair as he laps at my clenching pussy lips. Adding a finger, he thrusts into me, elevating my desire and the sound of my moans. My orgasm comes quickly, and I shudder through it, my fists gripping his hair. Lowering my leg, he wipes at his mouth, the corner lifting as he watches me sit up with a satisfied grin.

"We can make cookies anytime you want if that's included."

Putting his hands on my waist, he helps me off the counter.

"If you think my mouth is skilled, wait until you experience what else I can do."

With my arms around his neck, I tilt my chin up and kiss him.

"That's what I'm afraid of. I can see myself easily getting addicted to the pleasure you give."

The soothing caress of his hands is on my back, kneading into my muscles.

"I enjoy pleasuring you, but I don't want you to think sex is all I care about. I care about you far more."

My fear is happening. I'm falling for Jaxson, and I don't believe any amount of willpower can stop it.

$\mathcal{I}$'m finishing wrapping the presents I bought when Jaxson enters my room, munching on the cookies we made last night.

"These are the best cookies ever."

"It's my grandmother's recipe. She was a gifted baker."

"She handed the skill down to you. Every time you bring something baked into the office, I skip lunch so I can eat a bunch of it."

Chuckling, I smile up at him.

"Thank you."

With my thumb on the wrapping paper, I stretch my arm out for the tape. Jaxson leans down and hands it to me.

"My friend, Joe is having a Christmas party tonight. Will you come with me?"

"Yes. Do I need to dress up?"

"Yeah, it's an ugly sweater party. Do you have one?"

"Actually, I do. Sasha hosted one last year. I kept it just in case."

"Great. Will you help me pick one out?"

Setting the taped box aside, I reach up and steal the half cookie from his hand. "Yep." Grinning, I stuff it in my mouth.

With a chuckle, he stands and offers his hand to me.

"Where do we go shopping for one?"

"A few stores will have some. You mind if we stop by the post office before shopping?"

"Not at all."

Jaxson helps me put the packages in totes before we head out to shop. A few hours later, we get back in time to shower and change. Leaving the bathroom, he enters my room as I'm putting on my knee-high boots over my leggings. Laughter ripples my belly as I take in his new look—a bright green sweater with a big lighted Santa face. The lights are battery operated and go through a series of twinkle modes. Above his sweater is a red, lopsided Santa hat. He looks ridiculous, yet he's still cute.

"Will Joe have food there or should we get something on the way?"

As I pass him, he flicks one of the dangling bulbs on my green garland Christmas tree sweater.

"His girlfriend is making food."

Going to the door, Jaxson reaches out for my jacket and holds it for me to slip into it.

"How is it you can wear a silly Christmas tree sweater and still look hot?"

"It's the bulbs. They lure all the men."

Jaxson laughs, putting his arm around me as we exit.

"I'll have to keep you close then."

A short taxi ride later, we're stepping onto the sidewalk in front of another apartment building, the front doors decorated with green garland and gold bulbs along the arch above them. On the fifth floor, we exit the elevators to the same decorative theme. Following Jaxson to one of the doors, I hear Christmas music thumping inside. Jaxson knocks, and a moment later, a tall, ginger-haired man with a full, red glittery beard opens the door. Jaxson laughs and clasps hands with the guy as he hugs him.

"Joe, this is Sophia."

Joe spreads his long arms and brings me in for a tight squeeze.

"Sophia! Welcome! I've heard a lot about you."

My stomach flutters that Jaxson has spoken with his best guy friend about me.

"I've heard a lot about you too. It's nice to meet you."

Jaxson takes my coat and purse and puts them in a closet with his jacket. Ushering me into his spacious, open concept apartment, Joe hands me a freshly made cup of Christmas punch. A tall, beautiful brunette comes up behind Joe, passes him, and heads toward

Jaxson. There's something familiar about the woman; I'm pretty sure I've seen her in our office before.

"Jaxson!"

She outstretches her arms and loops them around his neck. The sight tightens my chest, a prickle of jealousy forming in my gut. He makes an *oomph* sound and steps back, bringing her arms down.

"Hey, Claire."

"I missed you!"

It's clear the woman has had a couple cups of Christmas punch already. Her voice rises an octave, and she's not shy about groping her hands all over Jaxson. Obviously, they've had an intimate relationship before.

"Okay, that's nice," Jaxson replies, his gaze glancing my direction. "I'm here with someone. I'd like you to meet—" He points in my direction, but she lowers his arm and brings it up to her chest, cupping it against her breasts.

My eyes roll at the scene. This woman knows how to flirt and keep a man's attention—a skill I don't have. I'm no competition. Turning to Joe, I look away as my eyes moisten.

"Your apartment is nice. Does your girlfriend live here too?"

With sympathy coating his green irises, Joe's gaze pulls from Jaxson and Claire to me.

"Yeah, I'll introduce you."

Joe walks me over to the balcony doors and puts an

arm around a short, cute blonde. She's curvy in all the right places, and her big brown, doe eyes are above a bubbly, bright smile.

"Sarah, this is Sophia. Jaxson's roommate and co-worker I told you about."

"Welcome to our party," she says as she hugs me.

With the two of them next to each other, you can see a foot difference in height. It's adorable how little she is and how he looks at her with loving affection.

"Thank you. The ugly sweater theme was a great idea."

Sarah points to Joe's sweater, with a nude Santa holding a present in front of him that reads, *I have a big package for you.*

"He needed an excuse to wear this sweater," Sarah jokes.

Joe shrugs with a grin.

"We'll be doing a few sweater contests later. You can put your vote in the boxes over there." She points to the food-covered dining table with a few decorative boxes in the center of them. Each box has Post-its and pens next to them and a label on a box for each sweater contest.

As she lowers her hand, a guy with a light brown trimmed beard and messy blond hair joins our group. His sweater is playful with a Velcro bullseye in the center and soft balls sticking to it. It reads, *You miss, you drink.*

"Would you like to play with my balls?" he asks me.

I almost spit my drink out laughing. He points to his shirt and smirks.

"It got you laughing. My name is Devin."

He puts out his hand to shake.

"If you want to play, you can, or I can get us both another drink."

I raise my nearly empty cup and finish it off. "I'll play."

Devin's mouth tilts as he pulls three balls off his sweater and hands them to me.

"How far away should I be?"

Devin steps back a couple of feet and gives a thumbs up. Throwing the first ball, I laugh as it hits him in the chest and falls to the floor. Devin shrugs.

"Two more."

I toss the second ball, and it bounces off his sweater right about where his dick would be.

"Were you aiming for it?" he quips.

Laughing, I toss the third, and it sticks to the bottom of the bullseye. He picks up the other two balls.

"I'd still like to get you that drink."

Jaxson approaches from my right, carrying two drinks. Handing me one, he puts an arm around my waist and kisses my head. Even though I'm irritated about what I saw when we arrived, it doesn't stop the flutter of butterflies his affection creates.

"Hey, Devin," Jaxson nods, his expression serious. "I see you've met Sophia."

"Yeah, I was offering her a drink, but it looks like

you got that handled," Devin frowns. "It was good to meet you." Looking defeated, he walks off toward the punch bowl.

"I can't leave you alone, huh?"

"You were busy with your *friend*, so I was making my own. So, who is Claire?"

Jaxson rakes a hand down the side of his face and blows out a breath.

"She's someone I dated not too long ago, who I'm not interested in rekindling things with *at all*."

"She didn't get the memo."

"She has it now. I can't handle her level of cling. Seriously, Soph, it was overload. Multiple texts a day and wanted to talk on the phone before going to bed *every night*." His eyes widen in emphasis.

"Aww, you didn't want to soothe her into sleep with your sexy voice?" My tone is mocking, and it makes his mouth tilt.

"You think my voice is sexy?"

"Oh, jeez. Get over yourself."

Jaxson laughs as he leans forward and kisses my forehead.

"Gather around," Sarah calls to everyone. "Pick a partner. Someone you know."

Jaxson puts his hand on my lower back and pulls me closer. Sarah hands out sheets of paper and pens to her right, and they're passed around until everyone has one.

"This is a drinking game and will show how well

you know your partner. The more you miss, the more you drink," she says as she grins.

Jaxson looks at me and winks, then starts in on his sheet. The sheet has ten questions. After writing your partner's name, you have to answer the questions about them—their favorite Christmas drink, their favorite Christmas movie, their favorite Christmas cookie… I go through them, answering them pretty easily, only one making me think hard.

Ten minutes later, Sarah calls time. "Let's see how well you did. Hand your sheet to your partner so they can mark if it's correct or not. Every time it's wrong, take a drink!"

Jaxson and I swap sheets, and I watch him go through my sheet. Raising his pen, he puts an X next to the question, *Where would your partner spend Christmas if they had the choice to go anywhere?*

Jaxson lifts the sheet and faces it toward me, tapping on the bottom of it. "You missed one. Take a drink." He nods to my cup, and I lift it, swallowing down the sweet liquid.

"What's the right answer?"

Shrugging a shoulder, he holds my gaze as his softens. "I wouldn't go anywhere else. I'm spending Christmas where I want to be, with you."

"You really mean that?"

"I mean it." Taking my hand, he brings me closer so he can put his arms around my back. "I'm looking forward to celebrating Christmas with you."

"Jaxson."

"What?"

Blowing out a breath, I don't know what to do about my rapid beating heart, the warm sensation spreading through my body and my clouded mind.

"You didn't miss any of the questions about me."

"I know. No one knows you better than I do."

I'm held against his warm chest as he hugs me. Over his shoulder, I notice Devin and Claire partnered up. They're both repeatedly taking drinks. Chuckling, I turn Jaxson toward them.

"Look."

"That's a perfect match," Jaxson laughs. "He clearly likes things that cling to him."

Tapping his shoulder, I giggle.

"You want to get something to eat, then vote on sweaters?"

"Yeah."

Tossing the papers in the trash, we move over to the table, and he hands me a plate before taking one for himself. Gathering up a plateful of finger foods and pasta, we sit at the empty table next to the food table. Joe fills a plate too and sits across from Jaxson.

"Hey, man, Sarah wants to plan a New Year's Eve party. You two should come."

Jaxson bumps my shoulder and winks. "You want to go with me?"

The corner of my mouth lifts that his first thought is to bring me. "Yes."

"Great!" Joe claps his hands together. "I'm glad you came, Sophia. I was beginning to think you were a figment of Jax's imagination."

Joe winks, and there's a private exchange that passes between them as they look at each other. Jaxson laughs to himself.

"No, she's real."

"And just as beautiful as you said."

Remembering Jaxson's phone call, I wonder if it was Joe he was talking to.

"Thank you."

Jaxson smiles as he puts an arm around me. The three of us work at cleaning off our plates as a couple of Joe's guests belt out karaoke to a Christmas song. When we finish eating, Jaxson sits back and pats his belly. Moving his hand, I take over rubbing. Adoration fills his eyes as he strokes his hand over my loosely curled hair.

"Would you both like to go ice-skating tomorrow? Sarah wants to go, and if you like skating, Sophia, it'll give me and Jax the opportunity to stand on the side and drink beer. What do you say?"

Joe smooths his thumb and finger over his beard, shedding sparkles all over his empty plate and table beneath it. Laughing, I nod.

"Yes, I'll assist in your beer-drinking endeavors."

"I knew I'd like you."

While Joe and Jaxson chat, I take our plates and toss them. At the food table, I think about my votes for the sweater contest and write them on the post-its, fold them, and drop them in. The guys are still chatting when I'm done, so I get another drink and admire the view from Joe and Sarah's balcony doors. Claire steps up next to me, scrutinizing me with narrowed lids.

"It won't last with him. Sarah tried to warn me, and I didn't listen."

My stomach knots as I avoid looking at her flawless face. "Mmm-hmm."

"He's a gorgeous heartbreaker with commitment issues."

"I'm not his girlfriend," I bite back. "I'm his best friend and roommate… and coworker."

"So, you're the reason I wasn't allowed to visit him at his workplace?"

"What do you mean?" My brows pinch inward as I glance at her smoky eyes.

"He didn't like me showing up there. He told me not to. It made me think he was sleeping with someone at work too."

Ugh. *Too.* Of course, he slept with her. Why wouldn't he? He was dating her, and she's stunning, but I still hate hearing it.

"It's none of your business, but we've never slept together."

"Well, once you do, he'll drop you just like he dropped me. It's all about the chase for guys like him, and once the chase is over, you're no longer exciting."

There's a war inside me, and it's not over a ten-day

bet. I believe I can hold out ten days and not sleep with Jaxson, but Mick was right, it's only a matter of time before the opportunities of living together encourage the attraction we have for one another. I'm slipping right into where I never wanted to be—the territory of friends with benefits.

"Thanks for the girl chat."

"Don't say I didn't warn you."

She saunters off, and I lower my head as my stomach churns with nausea. In my periphery, Jaxson is standing by the table, facing me. Approaching, concern fills his eyes and tightens his jaw.

"What did she say to you?"

"Nothing I didn't already know."

"Like what?"

When I look away, he takes my hand in his.

"Soph."

"My stomach is upset. I'm going to head home early."

"I'll go with you."

Withdrawing my hand from his, I shake my head. "You should stay and enjoy the party. I'll see you back home." Walking away from him, I hurry to the closet and gather my jacket and purse.

Glancing back over my shoulder, Jaxson's expression is pained as he watches me leave.

axson enters my room the next morning with a smoothie and sets it on my nightstand. Dropping onto my bed, he fills the opposite side as he lays his head on the pillow and gazes at me with his gorgeous hazel eyes.

"The party sucked after you left. I came back shortly after you, but you were already asleep."

Guilt is like a thorn in my side, prickly and sharp. I hadn't been asleep. I was in bed reading, but when I heard the front door open, followed by his footsteps, I turned the lamp off and pretended to be asleep to avoid talking.

"I'm sorry I ruined your night."

"You didn't ruin my night. Claire ruined it when she said something that upset you. Are you ready to tell me what she said?"

"She warned me not to enter into a relationship

with you and told me if I did, you'd get bored with me after we had sex and move on to someone else."

There's a tick in his jaw as his nostrils flare. Reaching out, he takes my hand.

"Come here." Lying on his back, he brings me atop him, his hand caressing my hair. "You're not a fling. You're not someone I'm trying to get to know only to learn things that drive me crazy. You're the one woman I've always been able to be myself around, to joke with, to ask for ideas and help. The only thing you've ever judged me for is my sex life, and it's the same reason I hassle you about every guy you date."

As he stares up at me, caressing my face and hair, I can sense my wall crumbling.

"You wanted me once, and I messed it up. I'm not going to mess up again. Our friendship isn't enough. I want more, Sophia. I want you."

Lowering into his arms, I let go, allowing my emotions to freefall. I'm as terrified as I am thrilled about the possibilities. I tried all night to make excuses why I shouldn't be with him, but they all dissolve when his lips press to mine. Despite my fears, giving my heart to Jaxson is the only thing that feels right.

Turning us, he puts me on my back and sits upright. Unbuttoning my pink button-down nightgown, he opens the fabric. With his arm holding him up, he brings his lips to my breast, sucks my nipple into his mouth, teasing it until it's swollen, and my body is aching with need. Moving the fabric away from my hips, he slides a hand into my underwear. Wet with desire, he coats his fingers as he swirls them around my clit. Moving his fingers down, he slides them into me, and I arch my back as the pleasure rushes over me.

"I have a confession," he whispers between nipping my breast.

"What is it?"

"When I decorated your room, I might've done some snooping and found your vibrator."

My mouth curls, knowing the reason he snooped is that he wanted to know what toys I had. Thrusting harder, he works me toward an orgasm as I look up at him and his wayward grin.

"I want to use it on you. Will you let me?"

Putting my hand over his, I keep him at the angle he's at, and he keeps his pace.

"Yes," I whisper between moans.

"Yes, on the vibrator, or yes, you want to come?"

"Both."

He withdraws his fingers, and I whimper. That widens his grin as he opens the drawer of my nightstand. Pulling out the blue, lifelike vibrator, he turns the knob at the end, starting the vibration as I remove my underwear. With his hand on the inside of my thigh, he spreads my legs and places the head of the vibrator at my opening. Moving it up and down, he rubs it along my clit and pussy lips, ensuring I'm ready. As my moans increase, he pushes it in, pulls out, then pushes further in. He repeats, and each time, he angles it up to press against my G-spot. Quickening his pace, he leans down and sucks my nipple, adding to the pleasure that's reaching its crest. Gripping his shoulder, my body shakes as I reach my orgasm. Smiling, he covers my lips with his.

Turning the knob to off, he drops the vibrator to the side as he lowers himself on top of me, keeping our kiss going, prolonging the pleasure tingling through my body. My hands go to his pants, and he reaches down to help remove them. Kicking them and his briefs off, he moves farther up and straddles my chest. Leaning over, he grips the bed frame as I take his erection in my mouth. As I suck, he thrusts into my mouth and throat, then back out. With each thrust, he holds his hand over mine at the base of his cock while the other makes the bed frame creak with the strength of his grip. Several more thrusts, and he slows as his cock thickens. Warm cum fills my mouth, and I swallow before he pulls out.

Dropping onto his back, he exhales a breath as he puts his arm over his head. His other arm curls around me as I lie on his chest.

"That was hot, so fucking hot." Putting his fingers through my hair, he brings the other hand down and presses his finger on my bottom lip. "This mouth is capable of bringing me to my knees. I'll do anything to feel these lips."

Twirling my fingers on his muscled chest, my mouth curls.

"It turns me on how much you enjoy it."

Turning us to our side, he props his head on his hand and bent elbow as he caresses along my side.

"Is there anything that's off-limits? Anything you don't want me to do to you?"

"I'm not into being hurt or humiliated during sex."

Gathering my hand in his, he kisses my fingertips.

"Good, because I could never hurt you. What about anal?"

With a wink, I grin.

"Yes, I'm into it."

"Fuck, yes." Leaning forward, he smiles against my lips as he kisses me. "What's your favorite position?"

"Doggy style or me on top. Both hit my G-spot the best. What about you?"

"I won't know until I do all of them with you." There's a wicked glimmer in his eyes as his mouth upturns. "What about having sex in public places? How do you feel about that?"

"It's a turn on, but some places are too public."

"I agree with both. How about at work?"

"We can't make it a habit because sooner or later, we might get caught."

"It's going to be very difficult for me not to bend you over your desk, lift your skirt, and have my way with you."

My cheeks warm as my stomach flutters.

"It's going to be difficult not to *let* you have your way with me."

71

"We'll have to find excuses for late-night work sessions, so I can pleasure you before we come home."

Putting my hand on his cheek, I lean in to kiss him. "I'd like that."

Lying on my back, my mouth curls in response to the joy I feel.

"We did this backward. We're supposed to date, then move in with each other later. We went for moving in together first before you became my boyfriend."

Jaxson lies above me, grazing his spread fingers between my breasts as he watches my eyes.

"Am I? Your boyfriend?"

"It doesn't feel right to say we're just dating."

"Because we aren't." His lips feather kisses along my stomach, and it stirs my arousal. "We're in a relationship."

"What makes it a relationship?"

Coming back up, he licks my nipple, then kisses my breast, sending goosebumps along my arms.

"I don't want to be with anyone else, and I definitely don't want you dating anyone else."

Taking his hand, I put it between my legs.

"I don't want you to date anyone else either. I want you all to myself."

Sliding a finger into me, he thrusts slowly.

"You have me."

❄

In the park, an ice rink has been set up along with booths for vendors, food, and drinks; the leafless trees filled with sparkling white lights give a romantic and festive atmosphere to the snow-covered surroundings. Walking hand in hand, Jaxson leads me to where we're meeting Joe and Sarah. At the edge of the rink, we see them ahead and wave. Joe notices our hands together and grins. It's a different look, seeing him without a glitter-filled beard.

Sarah gives me a hug when we reach them.

"I'm glad you guys came."

She and I head to the rink stand, Joe and Jaxson following behind.

"Do you like to skate?"

"Yeah, it's been a year or so since I've done it, but I think I'll pick it back up quickly."

"Oh, good. This will be fun."

As we approach the stand, the guys catch up and purchase our tickets. Jaxson gets mine and kisses me when I try to protest. Sitting on a bench, I push my feet into the skates while Jaxson locks our shoes in one of the lockers in front of us. Sitting next to me, he puts on hockey skates.

"Are you comfortable on skates?"

"I am, but it's been a while."

When I stand, Jaxson puts his hands on either side of me in case I lose my balance. With success, I'm able to balance on the blades and make it to the rink. Jaxson takes my hand as I wobble onto the ice, then slowly move my feet forward. It takes a few minutes before muscle memory kicks in and I'm gliding smoothly. Jaxson releases my hand, turns, and skates backward while holding my hands.

"Showing off those hockey skills is pretty sexy."

Glancing over his shoulder, he makes sure there's no one for us to run into.

"I was hoping it would impress you."

"It worked. When is your and Joe's next game?"

"After Christmas. Would you like to come?"

"Yes." My brows knit together. "Will that make me a puck bunny?"

Jaxson slows us, lets go of one of my hands, and spins me. Bringing me into his arms, he propels us forward as I skate backward, my balance kept steady with the strength of his arms.

"Are you there for me or the game?"

"You. The game is a bonus."

"Technically, that makes you my puck bunny."

"Should I get a cute costume and ears for some role play?"

Jaxson laughs, and it vibrates across my chest, making me laugh.

"You would look sexy in a pink one-piece and stockings. The ears would have to go pretty quick, though. They'd ruin it for me."

When I laugh, his smile widens, and he leans down to kiss me.

"I love seeing you smile."

"I feel the same about you. You practically melt my panties with that naughty grin of yours."

"I need to up my game because I want your panties fully melted."

My back gently meets the wall of the rink. Putting my hands on his fleece sweater, I latch onto the muscles beneath it as he holds me up in his arms. Leaning down, he slips his tongue between my lips. Weakening my knees, he fills our kiss with passion, the movement of his lips expressing how much he wants me.

Skates skid to a stop next to us. "Easy, Romeo. You're gaining an audience," Joe teases.

Jaxson pulls back and my lips tingle for more. My body is warmer, the cold air forgotten. Giving one last kiss, Jaxson releases his arms around me. Above his crimson cheeks, his lusty-filled eyes hold my gaze as he presses his thumb to my parted lips.

"I guess we'll have to behave until later."

With a wink, he skates backward and outstretches his hand for me to take it. Joe skates on the other side of him.

"I'm going to lose the skates and get some rum cider. You coming?"

Jaxson looks over at me, and I give an approving nod.

"Yeah, I'll join you."

With a kiss to my cheek, he leaves with Joe. Sarah skates up to my side, and we continue skating together around the circle.

"It looks like you guys are having fun."

"We are. I'm glad Joe invited us."

"Me too."

"It was a fun party you hosted yesterday. I had a nice time, and it's been great getting to know you and Joe."

A frown tugs at her lips.

"I'm sorry about what my friend Claire said to you at the party. Joe told me Jaxson was really upset you left the party after your conversation. I don't want what she said to ruin things. Jaxson is crazy about you. He's had feelings for you for a long time."

A swirl of butterflies flap in my stomach.

"What do you mean?

"I probably shouldn't tell you this, but I'm worried Claire put doubt in your mind. Jaxson has wanted to date you for a while. I'd hear Jaxson telling Joe about how you broke it off with a guy you were dating, and sure enough, Jaxson would dump the woman he was seeing. It didn't matter who he dated. They were never you."

Putting my hand on her arm, I stop us by the rink wall. Speechless, I stare at her soft chocolate eyes as she looks back at me worried.

"I shouldn't have said anything."

"No, I'm glad you told me. It... it explains a lot. I really needed to hear it."

We push off the wall and continue circling the rink.

In my chest, my heart is leaping, and through every limb, my body tingles with warmth.

"Why didn't he ever tell me?"

Sarah snorts. "His ego."

Nodding, I laugh to myself. "That makes sense."

"I'm sure he was afraid of rejection or losing you as a friend if it got awkward. You know how guys are. They can make the first move sexually but not emotionally."

"What's ironic is I've had a crush on him for three years. I hated seeing him date other women."

"Oh my." Sarah rubs across her brow. "So, neither of you admitted your feelings."

"Nope."

"Well, now you can change that."

Joe and Jaxson approach the side of the rink and wave us over. Stopping against the wall, I lean forward and accept Jaxson's kiss.

"Would you like some?"

Holding his cup out for me, I take it and sip the warm cider. It soothes the chill on my back and adds to the warmth I feel on the inside.

"Do you still want to skate?"

"No." I hand the drink back to him. "I'm ready to take them off and be with you."

"Good. I'll meet you at the lockers."

Sarah and I skate there slowly. The guys catch up and take our hands to help us to the benches. Jaxson squats down in front of me and unties my laces. The sweet gesture draws my lips to his.

"Thank you."

"Of course."

I hold on to his cider as he brings me my shoes. Taking a drink, I hand it back to him, and he gathers my skates to take back to the rink stand. When he returns, I'm finished putting my shoes on, and he takes my hand as I stand.

As the four of us walk through the food stands, Jaxson lets go of my hand and puts his arm around me when a chill hits me. Rubbing his hand up and down my side, he tries to warm me, then hands me his drink.

"Here. Have the rest. It'll warm you up."

"Thank you."

Sarah points to a booth selling chimney cakes.

"That's where I'm headed."

Jaxson and I follow and stand in line behind them.

"You want to share one?" Jaxson asks.

"Oh yeah."

Joe and Sarah get their order first, find a picnic table nearby, and we join them on the opposite side. Peeling a piece off our chimney cake, I hold it up for Jaxson, and he licks my finger as he takes it. Peeling off another piece, he holds it up for me. When I take it from his hand, I lick his finger, and his eyes glimmer with lust. Putting his hands on the outside of my thighs, he moves me closer between his legs.

"We should head home soon."

Leaning next to his ear, I lower my voice. "You want my lips around your thick cock, don't you?"

The hand on my hip lowers and squeezes my ass.

"And if I do?"

"Then you're in for a better treat than this cake."

Nibbling my ear, he bites it before sucking the lobe into his mouth, the sensation building my already growing arousal.

"We should go."

"Let's finish this cake, then say goodbye to them."

With a nod, he caresses his thumb into the nook of my thigh, the teasing touch making me ache for more.

Coming through the front door of our apartment, we can't get each other's clothes off fast enough. On the way to my room, he tosses his shirt with mine. In the hall, we leave my bra and his jeans. In my room, he strips me out of my pants and underwear, removes his, then lifts my legs, and tosses me on the bed.

Falling above me, he crashes his lips to mine, his hand curling in my hair as his other holds my hip. Raising my knees, I wrap my legs around his waist, and he pushes his erection against my opening. Moaning, I grip his hair, and he pushes against me again, sliding up, then down, coating himself in my desire.

"If you want to stop, we have to now." His voice is strained as he pushes against me.

"Don't stop. I want you."

Rocking his hips back, he slides into me, filling me. Rolling his hips back, he comes forward, thrusting deeper, harder, gripping my hip as he thrusts again. Our lips unite, the passion between us electric. It courses through me, sparking every nerve ending and surging my heartbeat for the man I'm falling in love with. Another thrust and my body pulses, my orgasm spilling onto him as I hold him close and shiver with pleasure.

"Do I need to pull out?"

"No, I'm on the pill."

Slipping his fingers between mine, he holds my arm above my head as he tightens his grip on my hip and increases the pace and pressure of his thrusts. Another orgasm shapes my mouth into an "O" as the euphoric sensation travels through my body. Tightening his fingers with mine, he moans through his own orgasm, his thrusts slowing, then stopping as he eases his grip on my hip.

When he pulls out, he kisses me with affectionate tenderness. Caressing my cheek, he grazes his thumb over my lips and stares down at me with love in his eyes.

"Will you stay the night with me?" I ask, rubbing my fingers along his back.

"Yes. Tonight, and every night you want me to."

With another kiss, he lifts himself off me, then takes my hand and helps me off the bed. Folding the blanket down, he climbs in, then spreads out his arm and the blanket for me to join him.

We lie on our sides, my back to his front, his arm wrapped around me, holding me close to his chest. Lowering his hand, he massages his fingers against my clit, and I hiss from the intense desire that courses through me. Licking my ear, he moves my leg over his thigh, giving him better access to pleasure me. Sliding his fingers into me, he heightens my arousal, pushing my body toward another orgasm.

Sliding back, he spreads my leg wider by lifting his knee. From behind, he slides his cock into me and rocks my hip toward him as he thrusts in and out. Just when I feel another orgasm building, he pulls out, turns me onto my stomach, and jerks my ass into the air. Taking hold of my hips, he thrusts in hard, slapping my ass against his pelvis. Fisting the pillow, I moan into it as another orgasm makes my legs tremble. Holding me in place, Jaxson's breathing heightens as he pounds into me. With a groan of satisfaction, he releases into me.

He pulls out, and I drop onto my back, utterly exhausted. Sweat beading off his brow and chest, he wipes a droplet off his forehead. Dropping down next to me, he smiles against my lips as he kisses me.

"Don't plan on much sleep tonight."

"I don't think my body can take it," I grin.

"How about a shower and some hot tea? Then I'll

bend you over the couch, then you can ride me on the chair."

"Oh my God, you're insatiable." Biting my lip, I reach over and caress along his length. "Yes, I want all of that."

CHAPTER 9

*M*y body aches all over, but it was worth it. It was the hottest night of sex I've ever experienced. I had more orgasms in our single night than I've had in entire relationships. Rolling over, I put my hand on his chest and sigh. Waking up, he puts his hand over mine, a smile curling his lips.

"We're going to need a double dose of your energy smoothies this morning."

"I'm sore in parts of my body I was unaware could be sore."

"Was it worth it?"

"Completely."

Turning on his side, he leans forward to kiss me. Caressing my hair, he trails his hand down and over the curves of my body. The way he touches and admires me with affection steals my heart—he has it in his grip, and I never want him to let it go. But there's something I need to come clean about, and it needs to happen now.

"I have a confession to make."

His eyes snap to mine.

"What is it?"

"Mick made a bet with me."

His brow rises.

"Uh-huh?"

"He bet we couldn't live together and not have sex. Actually, his exact words were: a single guy and woman who are attracted to each other can't live together without having sex. I disagreed and took his bet. Ten days until Christmas, and if we had sex, I lost."

His caressing doesn't stop, and I'm relieved. He doesn't even look angry.

"How does it feel to have lost that bet?"

"My ego took a hit, but I wouldn't change anything, Jaxson." Stroking his chest, I lie over him, looking into the beautiful mixture of olive, gold, and caramel in his eyes. "I'm falling in love with you."

Lowering me to his lips, he moves his mouth with mine in a passionate and loving embrace. With a hand caressing over my shoulder and back, his lips curve as he stares up at me.

"It's always been you I wanted. I'm not letting anything get in the way anymore. You're all I want this Christmas and every Christmas after."

With his hand grazing my hip, he moves it across

my ass and tugs me against his growing erection as I lower myself to kiss him.

"Let's not go anywhere today. I want to spend it in bed with you."

Wrapping an arm around me, he lays me on my back and slides his cock across my opening, igniting my desire and sending a rush of pleasure throughout my body.

"I have no plans other than making love to you."

After choosing a movie from the TV app, I enter the kitchen as Jaxson is adding whipped cream and chocolate shavings to the dirty snowmen drink he discovered. It's a twist on hot cocoa, adding mint ice cream and Baileys Irish Cream. As he puts the whipped cream back in the fridge, he winks.

"We should save some of that for later."

"I like that idea."

Grinning, I gather one of the cups and follow him into the living room. Cup in hand, I nestle into his open arm on the couch.

"This looks amazing." Taking a sip, I find it tastes as flavorful and smooth as it looks. "Mmm, I love the chocolate shavings." Plucking one off the top, I toss it in my mouth.

The corner of his lips rises as he watches me.

Tightening his arm, he hugs me into his chest and kisses my head.

"You're so damn sexy."

Gathering a dollop of whipped cream on my finger, I bring it to his lips, and with a slow, sensual motion of his tongue, he licks it off, teasing my arousal.

"So are you."

"Are we going to make it through this movie?" He winks.

"Yes! My lady bits need a break from all the pounding they've taken."

"I'll give them a break for the night, but tomorrow, no holds barred. I'm claiming that pussy."

Covering my mouth, I hold back laughter and quickly swallow my mouthful.

"You know tomorrow is Mick's Christmas party, right?"

"He's going to know we're together pretty quick. I won't be able to keep my hands off you."

"He can keep my entire Christmas bonus. I don't care."

Setting his half-empty glass on the coffee table, Jaxson sits back, puts his arms around me, and leans me back against his chest as he caresses my stomach.

"It makes me feel good to hear that."

"Good. Because I can't express how much you mean to me, not in words."

"The more we're together, the more I feel it." His warm hand rubs along my arm as he kisses my cheek.

"Jaxson…"

"Yeah?"

Sitting up, I set the cup down on the coffee table next to his and turn sideways to face him.

"The last few days have been better than any relationship I've had before. I imagined us being together, but my fantasies didn't come close to how amazing it is to be with you."

Putting his hand to my cheek, he caresses it.

"This is just the beginning. We have so much more to experience together."

"I'm looking forward to all of it."

"I am too."

CHAPTER 10

*C*arrying a bottle of wine with a bow around it, I walk up the steps to Mick's townhouse. The front door has a beautiful, enormous white and gold wreath on it, and once Mick opens his door, I admire the same white and gold theme extravagantly decorated throughout their home. Mick waves us in, and I hand him the wine bottle.

"I'm glad you both could make it." With a finger, he points to the closet to the left of us. "You can put your coats in there."

Entering the living room, we greet his wife and our co-workers. Anya, Mick's wife, fills two glasses with cranberry cocktails and brings them to us. With her cooking and baking skills, I'm not surprised the drink is delicious. Anya's wearing a beautiful white cocktail dress that flatters her curves and long dark hair. Knowing this party would be dressier, I chose a red, fitted, mid-thigh cocktail dress with a square neckline and plunging V back down to my hips.

Jaxson's hand rests on my lower back, caressing me affectionately as we drink and talk with the others. Mick notices Jaxson's hand on my back and his mouth curls.

"It looks like the roommate situation is working out."

"It is. Jaxson's been great. I wish he'd been my roommate sooner." I give Jaxson a sideways glance, and he grins behind the rim of his glass.

"So do I," he replies.

Mick smiles before tilting his glass back but doesn't say anything.

"Dinner is ready," Anya announces, clasping her hands in front of her. "Let's move into the dining room."

As we move through the rooms in the house, I admire the elegant decorations. There's no doubt in my mind the ornaments, garland, and trees have been professionally placed. Entering the dining room, the table setting is just as extravagant with white and gold plates, sparkling silverware, wine glasses, and candlelit centerpieces.

Jaxson pulls a chair out for me, and I graze my hand along the shimmery ribbon tied around it before sitting.

"Everything looks beautiful," I compliment Anya.

Her eyes light up as she takes the end seat next to Mick, who's at the head of the table.

"Thank you. This is our first year using a commercial decorator, and I'm pleased with their work."

"They did a great job."

"Saves her the time of putting up decorations; that way, she can enjoy cooking and party planning," Mick tells us.

"See now, that's love. You're making things easier for her."

Anya puts her hand over Mick's, and the two look at each other adoringly.

"He's the best," she proclaims.

Jaxson places his hand on my thigh and gives it a gentle squeeze. My eyes meet his, and he caresses my leg, the corner of his mouth rising as his eyes fill with adoration. Putting my hand over his, I caress it.

"I'll get the bottle of wine," Anya announces, breaking Jaxson and my attention from one another.

Mick pats her hand and stands. "I'll get it."

The rest of their guests have gathered around the long, twelve-chair table. The only people I know are two co-workers, Chris and Rayna, and they've taken the seats next to Jaxson. Chris does coding while Rayna is technical customer service. We're the only employees Mick has in his successful software and consulting business.

Jaxson and Chris enter into a discussion that

involves their expertise in eMarketing and coding. Tuning them out, I turn my attention to Anya.

"Thank you for having us over for dinner."

"Of course. All of you help make this possible, so the least we can do is invite you over for a delightful meal and entertainment."

Anya is so prim and proper, I have a hard time imagining her in a collar, on all fours, yipping, howling, or whatever crazy dog sounds she'd make. The thought turns my cheeks red, and I'm grateful Mick returns with the wine just then. Raising my glass, I accept his offer of wine and drink enthusiastically in an attempt to forget the images gallivanting through my mind.

With our glasses full, the guests nibble on the appetizers while Mick and Anya bring in the Christmas dishes. Mick slices the ham and places some on everyone's plates. With side dishes added, our conversations slow as we enjoy the delicious food. Conversation picks back up when the desserts are served. I barely ate all day, so I could enjoy Anya's desserts. First, it's the red velvet cake, and as I spoon a mouthful, I moan.

Jaxson looks over at me, his brow rising as his mouth twists up.

"Like that, do you?"

"Goodness, yes."

With another bite, I moan again, and Jaxson's hand slides up my thigh as he leans over to my ear.

"You're giving me a hard-on moaning like that."

"I can't help moaning when something gives me pleasure," I whisper back.

Grazing my ear with his tongue, he moves his hand farther up my thigh, quickly swiping his fingers along my underwear, exciting my desire for him. Removing his hand, he sits back in his chair and watches as my cheeks grow warm. My eyes widen, and I give him a pointed look.

"Behave," I giggle.

With a naughty grin, Jaxson throws an arm around my chair, and Mick's attention goes right to it. He and Mick look at each other, and something passes between them, leaving me with a question for later.

As dinner finishes, more desserts are brought into the living room as we gather in it. Anya stands by the tree and gathers our attention.

"We have a few games planned if you're sticking around. We'll be doing an ornament guess." She points to the ten-foot, elegant white and gold Christmas tree that looks like it easily has three hundred ornaments on it. "Closest guess gets a fifty-dollar gift card," she enthuses. "Then we'll play a game of Two Truths and One Lie, followed by Christmas charades if we're good and tipsy."

No one makes any effort to leave, so Anya hands out little pieces of paper and pens. Jaxson quickly writes a number on it and tosses it into the basket being passed around. With the pen to my lips, I stare at the tree, trying to get a good look and guess at how many there are. Writing down 275 and my name, I toss the paper and pen into the basket.

The basket is returned to Anya, and she opens the pieces of paper and reads them aloud.

"The winner is Rayna with her guess of two hundred and seventy-eight. There are two hundred and eighty-two ornaments."

"So close," I whine.

"What'd you guess?" Jaxson asks.

"Two seventy-five."

Anya picks a gift card off their coffee table and hands it to Rayna. Motioning her hands, Anya offers for us to sit on the couches and chairs. Jaxson and Chris sit on either side of me on one of the couches while others fill in the rest of the seats.

"Make sure your glasses are full, and we'll begin with Mick," Anya smiles. "He'll say two truths and one lie. If the person next to him guesses which is a lie, Mick has to drink. If you don't guess right"—she points to Sheila sitting left of Mick—"then you drink. The game will continue in a circle with the person to the left of you guessing your lie."

With nods, we give our understanding.

"All right," Mick begins, looking at Sheila. "Anya and I have vacationed in Denver, Colorado. My right leg is shorter than my left leg. I have never been on a rollercoaster."

"Ooh, those are good," Sheila retorts.

Smiling behind my glass of wine, I keep quiet. I

know he has one leg shorter than the other and wears specially ordered shoes, and I also know he's been on a rollercoaster because his family went to Disney, and he said he and his kids enjoyed the Forbidden Mountain rollercoaster at Animal Kingdom.

"You've never been on a rollercoaster?" Sheila questions with hesitation.

"Incorrect," Mick replies. "We have not vacationed in Denver, Colorado. Drink up." Mick grins.

The next few guests take their turn, then it's my turn to guess Chris's lie.

"I'm colorblind. I have over ten plants in my house. I used to be afraid of elevators."

The elevator fear has to be true. I swear he cringes just before stepping into the elevator in our building. It's fifty-fifty on the other two.

"You don't have over ten plants in your house."

Chris takes a drink. "You're right. I don't have any."

"You don't have any in your office, so it was a guess you might not have any in your house."

"Good observation," he praises.

Looking at Jaxson, the corners of my mouth lift. This is going to be tough. He knows a lot about me.

"Ready?"

"Yeah," he grins.

"I've broken my wrist. I've never told a man, I love you. I hate dirty dishes in the sink."

Jaxson quirks a brow. "I know you don't like dirty dishes in the sink. You clean them right away." His brows tighten. "Hmm, the lie is you've never told a man, I love you."

"Wrong," I tip my wine glass toward his. "I've never broken either wrist. Drink."

Shock fills his face, and he dips his chin before lifting his glass.

"Really?" Rayna questions, surprise in her voice. "You've never said the *I love you* words?"

"No," I shake my head. "I take those words seriously. In all of my past relationships, I've never felt it was right to say them."

"She's waiting for the right guy," Mick chimes in. I catch him wink at Jaxson behind his wine glass, and now I know for sure there have been prior conversations between the two of them.

"Are you a virgin?" Rayna mouths, her dark, bouncy curls falling forward as she tilts her head and gives me wide eyes. Clearly, alcohol is making her more comfortable. She's not usually this outspoken.

"No, Rayna," I laugh. "I really enjoy sex."

A few chuckles ensue before glasses are lifted to mouths to hide their smiles. Jaxson's cheeks are a brighter hue, and I find it entertaining.

"Your turn." I pat Jaxson's leg.

Facing Anya, he begins. "When I was a kid, I wanted to be a hockey player. I used to have a crush on my ninth-grade English teacher. I dislike dogs."

Truth. Truth. Lie. I know he likes dogs and wants to get one. I also know he wanted to be a hockey

95

player growing up, and that's why he and Joe are in a hockey league together. Which leaves the truth about having a crush on his teacher. Giggling, I take a sip of my wine, and he glances at me with a knowing smirk.

"Mmm, the lie is about not liking dogs," Anya answers.

Jaxson takes a drink. "Correct."

"You're too nice of a guy not to like dogs," Anya adds.

"Which means he had a crush on his ninth-grade teacher," I laugh.

Jaxson watches me giggling, a humored smile lifting the corner of his mouth.

"What? She was really hot."

"I had a crush on one of my teachers too," Mick's friend, Rodney, shares. "Back then, the teachers always wore skirts. Her legs..." Rodney angles his head and blows out a breath. "They were long, lean, and attached to a hot ass."

As everyone laughs and his wife rolls her eyes, I leave the group to use the restroom before the next game begins. As I'm washing my hands, the door begins to open.

"Someone's in here."

The door opens wider, and Jaxson slips through, closing it behind him.

"I know." Putting his arms around my waist, he backs me toward the sink. Sliding his hands down, he cups my ass, my fingers gripping the collar of his shirt as he lifts me onto the counter.

"What's everyone doing?"

"Busy starting charades."

Lowering to my lips, he fuels my desire. Pressing his erection into me, I moan through our kiss.

"What if they hear us?"

"Then we need to be quiet."

"Are we really going to have sex in our boss's bathroom?"

Spreading my legs wider, he rubs his fingers against my clit through my underwear.

"Are you telling me to stop?"

"No." My hands reach for the button and zipper of his pants, hastily opening them and freeing him from his briefs. With his stretched cock in my hand, I guide it between my legs. Holding my underwear to the side, he thrusts into me and covers my mouth with his.

Slick heat warms me below as he holds my ass tight and pounds into me. Each moan I elicit is smothered by his passion-filled kiss.

Taking me harder, he keeps one hand around my ass as he grips the sink edge. Pleasure intensifying, I drop my head back as the sensation of an orgasm begins. The door cracks open, and my body tightens, my mounting orgasm fading. Mick catches sight of us, then chuckles as he closes the door.

"Lock it next time," he says through the door, his voice fading away.

"Oh my God." My face burns hot, no doubt red.

Jaxson laughs, reaches back, locks the door, then slowly increases his thrusts.

"He knows now for sure. No point in stopping."

With a giggle, I accept his kiss and grip his ass, tugging him, so his cock goes deeper. Smiling against my lips, he thrusts harder, working my pleasure back to its peak. He kisses along my cheek then my neck as I grip his arm and shoulder, shuddering through my orgasm. Several more thrusts, and he groans, resting his head against mine. Pulling out, he winks at me with a wicked grin.

"I love being with you."

"I feel the same."

Helping me down off the sink, he squeezes my ass, then adjusts himself, and tucks his dick back in his briefs.

"I'll go out first."

"That's fine. I need a minute to clean up."

He leaves, and I bite my lip as the residual pleasure lingers.

When I return to the living room, Mick smirks behind his fresh glass of wine as I sit next to Jaxson, who puts an arm around me. I give Jaxson a kiss on the cheek, and Chris and Rayna notice, their expressions showing their surprise.

Rayna points a finger between us.

"Are you two together?"

Jaxson, chin in his hand, smiles as he looks at me.

"Yes," I tell her. "We are."

"About damn time," Chris jokes.

"Mmm-hmm," Mick agrees.

"I always knew there was something between you two," Rayna shares. "It's good to see you both so happy."

Jaxson rubs my back, rests his hand at my neck, and brings me to him for a kiss. "Really happy," he says aloud, his eyes filled with adoration.

An hour later, Jaxson is holding my coat out for me to slip into it. Mick approaches us and shakes Jaxson's hand goodbye, then brings me in for a hug.

"Bets off," he whispers. Pulling back, he gives an approving nod to us. "It's good to see the two of you together. You have my approval."

Jaxson puts an arm around me. "Thanks for having us. We had a great time."

The corner of Mick's mouth rises. "I bet you did."

We share a smile, then take the other's hand as we leave.

CHAPTER 11

HRISTMAS DAY…

Hearing Jaxson enter my room, I turn over to face him. Laughter rolls out of my belly as he walks in with nothing but whipped cream on his cock and his lopsided Santa hat.

"That's sexy, baby."

"I thought you'd like it."

As he nears the bed, I sit up. Swiping my finger across the whipped cream, I gather some, and slowly lick it off my finger. Jaxson's cock rises, his erection growing.

"That all needs to come off before we have sex."

"I was hoping you'd help me with that."

He winks, and I lower my mouth, licking some of the whipped cream off of him.

"I'll definitely help you."

Gathering my hair, he holds it in his hand as I lick his cock, cleaning off the whipped cream. When enough is gone, I put him into my mouth and suck.

"Best Christmas ever," he says between moans.

Several thrusts into my mouth, and he's fisting my hair tighter as he reaches his orgasm. Stepping back, he places his hands on my arms and pulls me from the bed.

"Let's take a shower together."

Wrapping his hands around my ass, he lifts me. I put my legs around his waist as he carries me to the bathroom. Letting my legs down, he turns the knob on, removes his Santa hat, tossing it to the floor. Stepping into the shower first, he follows me in. Gathering soap in my hands, I lather his cock and clean it. Once he's rinsed, he places his hands on my ass, lifts my thighs, and wraps them around his waist. With my back against the wall, he kisses me into delirium as he thrusts into me. My back slides up and down the wall as he takes me harder, pounding against my G-spot, making me cry out as I reach my release.

Lowering my legs, he feathers kisses along my neck, bringing his lips to mine.

"Are you ready to open your presents?"

"Yes."

Together, we dry off, and I enter my room,

searching for my blue sweater and matching knee-high stockings. With no underwear on, I join him in the living room. He's making us hot chocolate and stops when he sees what I'm wearing.

"No underwear?"

I shake my head, and his mouth curls.

"Just how I like it."

Handing a mug to me, he puts a hand under my sweater as I begin to walk away and squeezes my ass. Biting my lip, I give him a wayward glance. On the couch, I snuggle against the back cushion and sip my hot chocolate as he gathers two boxes and brings them to me.

"Open this one first." Handing me a pretty blue box with a silver ribbon, he sits next to me. Untying the ribbon, I lift the lid, my eyes expanding as I stare down at a pair of white gold and diamond stud earrings.

"They're beautiful."

Removing them from the box, I put them on.

"How do they look?"

"You're already stunning, they just add to your beauty."

Coming forward, I hold his face in my hands.

"Thank you. I love them."

He nods to the second box.

"Not yet," I tell him. "Open one of yours. That one," I point to the five-and-a-half-foot box. With questioning eyes, he walks over to it and begins peeling the wrapping paper off. When it's off enough for him to see what's inside, a smile stretches across his face.

"You got me a hockey stick!"

"It's one of the new ones out."

"This is... this is perfect, Soph. Thank you."

Setting the box down, he comes over to the couch, takes my mug from my hand, and sets it on the coffee table. Sitting next to me, he hugs me, then kisses me with an expression of gratitude that seeps through his kiss.

"Open your second box," he insists.

"Okay."

I take the box he hands me and untie the gold bow from the red box. Lifting the cover, I discover a white-gold charm bracelet. Bringing the bracelet out of the box, I take a closer look at the charms—a cookie, key, locket, and a circle charm that reads, *Cherish The Memories* dangle from the sparkly chain. Opening the locket, I find my grandmother's initials. Tears fill my eyes as I look up at him.

"Jaxson, this is incredibly special." Touching my finger to the key, I hold it up. "What does the key represent?"

"The key is for giving me a key to your apartment, which opened the door for us to begin a relationship." Reaching into his pocket, he withdraws another charm. "I had to go back and get this one." He puts the tiny stocking in my hand. "This is for the first time we were intimate, and I knew I loved you."

Tears spill, trickling down my cheeks. Putting my hand on his face, I caress his cheek, looking into the eyes of the man my heart belongs to.

"I love you."

A brief smile raises the corner of his mouth before he gathers the bracelet and box to set on the coffee table. Lowering on top of me, he hugs me to him, kissing me with sensual affection.

"Every moment with you is a memory I never want to forget. I love you, Sophia."

EPILOGUE

*N*EARLY ONE YEAR LATER...

Entering Mick's office, I set a cream box with a red bow on his desk. "Merry Christmas."

Mick lifts the box and gives it a light shake. "What did you get me?"

Sitting in the chair across from him, I grin. "Open it and find out."

Pulling the bow off, he lifts the top, brings the card out, and reads the front.

"Isn't this wonderful?" He smiles. "You are cordially invited to the wedding ceremony of Jaxson Parker and Sophia Ward," he reads aloud.

"Look under the card." I point to the box, and he

looks down and lifts two tickets. "Season hockey tickets. What are these for?" he asks, surprised.

"You knew all along Jaxson and I had feelings for one another. It was your matchmaking, your insistence we live together that brought us together. Jaxson told me he'd confided in you how much he cared for me. That bet never mattered to you. You knew we'd be intimate because of how we felt about each other. So, we thought of a way to thank you, and this was the best we could think of—a gift that would keep giving and an activity we know you would enjoy."

Mick sets the tickets and invitation on his desk.

"This is a great gift, but the wedding invitation is even better. You two deserve happiness, and I'm grateful you found it with each other. The love you share is something special. I watched it blossom over three years, and when I saw the opportunity to bring you together, I had to take it."

"I'm thankful you did. He's the best thing that's ever happened to me."

Mick's mouth curls. "He said the same thing about you."

Thank you for reading Countdown to Christmas! I hope you enjoyed Sophia and Jaxson's Christmas love story. If their office romance warmed your heart and steamed up your Kindle, I recommend reading My Hot Boss next.

Prepare to have your heart stolen in this sexy, witty, and swoon-worthy office romance:

Emma Williams wanted a night of complete freedom, and Grayson Cole's charming words and sexy-as-sin kiss promised to give her what she needed, but instead, the evening ended in disaster. A month later, trouble walks through her office door, and Emma is introduced to the same seductively handsome man she couldn't forget, and now, he's her new boss. Undeniable attraction is something she doesn't need, not when she's up for a promotion for her dream job and recovering from a devastating breakup, but every time she's near him, he stirs a fire inside her too strong to control. Keeping it professional isn't an option when Grayson is determined to have her and knows how to satisfy her every desire.

"OMG, I could not put this down!! The chemistry the two of them share is ridiculously hot right from the beginning, but because the pair suffer heartbreak in the past, it has them questioning their feelings. Such a whirlwind romance that has you hooked from the start! I absolutely loved this book definite 5 Star MUST READ!!!!" ~ *Tracy & Helen's Romance Book Blog*

. . .

Wondering what other passionate romances are in my collection? Fall in love with a swoon-worthy cowboy in Fire on the Farm, or a charming and perfectly sculpted kickboxing instructor in Unbreak This Heart. Or take a ride on the wild side and begin the Kings MC Romances with Castle of Kings.

You're welcome to join my Facebook readers' group, Betty's Book Beauties and Bad Boys, to connect with me personally, enjoy the fun, exclusive giveaways, and sneak peeks of future books! I'm in there once a week hanging out with my readers. :)

Keep turning the pages if you want to check out my other sexy and suspenseful stories, where to stay connected with me, what signings I'll be at next, as well as two bonus drink recipes from the story!

If you enjoyed Countdown to Christmas, will you consider leaving a review? It's reviews from fans like you that help spread the word about my books, giving me the opportunity to keep writing them.

To book lovers everywhere;
you are my tribe
you make my dream possible
and for that
I thank you.

ALSO BY BETTY SHREFFLER

Kings MC Series

CASTLE OF KINGS

CLIPPED WINGS

KING OF KINGS (Coming Jan 2020!)

Standalone Contemporary Romances

FIRE ON THE FARM

MY HOT BOSS

UNBREAK THIS HEART

Crowned and Claimed Series

CLAIMED ROYALTY

TWICE CLAIMED

FOREVER CLAIMED

https://bettyshreffler.com/

ABOUT THE AUTHOR

Betty Shreffler is a USA Today and International bestselling author of romance. She writes sexy and suspenseful stories with hot alphas and kickass heroines with twists you don't expect. She also writes beautiful and sexy romances with tough women and their journeys at finding love. Betty is a mix of country, nerdy, sassy, sweet and a whole lot of sense of humor. If she's not writing or doing book events, you can find her snuggling with her fur babies watching a movie, enjoying wildlife behind the lens of a camera, hiking in the woods, or sipping wine behind a deliciously steamy book.

Sign up for Betty's newsletter

Join Betty's Facebook readers' group:
Betty's Book Beauties and Bad Boys

Visit Betty's website for signed paperbacks,
or see where she'll be for her next signing:
https://bettyshreffler.com/

amazon.com/author/bettyshreffler

BB bookbub.com/profile/betty-shreffler

facebook.com/authorbettyshreffler

instagram.com/betty_shreffler

DRUNK JACK FROSTIE RECIPE

INGREDIENTS
- 1 cup vodka
- 1 cup champagne
- 1/2 cup Blue Curacao
- 1/2 cup lemonade
- 3 cups ice
- Lemon wedge
- White sanding sugar

DIRECTIONS

1. In a blender, combine vodka, champagne, blue curacao, lemonade, and ice. Blend until combined.

2. Run a lemon wedge around the rim of each glass then dip in sanding sugar.
3. Pour frosties into rimmed glasses and serve immediately.

DIRTY SNOWMEN RECIPE

INGREDIENTS

1/4 cup melted chocolate, for rim
1/2 cup chocolate shavings
1/2 pint vanilla ice cream
2 cup hot chocolate
1/2 cup Baileys
Whipped cream for serving

DIRECTIONS

1. Pour melted chocolate and chocolate shavings into separate shallow dishes. Dip the rims of two mugs in melted chocolate then immediately dip in chocolate shavings.
2. Using a medium cookie scoop, add a few scoops of ice cream into each mug. Pour hot chocolate and Baileys on top.
3. Top with whipped cream and sprinkle with any extra chocolate shavings.

CPSIA information can be obtained
at www.ICGtesting.com
Printed in the USA
BVHW031141230920
589475BV00001B/114